ƐB

D0834854

WHEN THE DAFFODILS BLOOM AGAIN

As the new century dawns in the Welsh mining village of Cwmbran, the Rees family faces many difficulties. When Davey Rees elopes with Verity Morgan, the colliery owner's daughter, the family stands to lose their home and livelihood. Meanwhile, Davey's sister Gwen loves Bryn Edwards, headmaster of the school where she teaches. Her hopes are dashed when he leaves Cwmbran to take up a teaching post in rural Canada. Will she ever see him again?

Books by Catriona McCuaig
in the Linford Romance Library:

CATRIONA McCUAIG

WHEN THE DAFFODILS BLOOM AGAIN

Complete and Unabridged

LINFORD
Leicester

First published in Great Britain in 2001

First Linford Edition
published 2007

British Library CIP Data

McCuaig, Catriona
    When the daffodils bloom again.—
    Large print ed.—
    Linford romance library
    1. Wales—Fiction
    2. Love stories
    3. Large type books
    I. Title
    823.9'2 [F]

    ISBN 978–1–84617–989–1

Published by
F. A. Thorpe (Publishing)
Anstey, Leicestershire

Set by Words & Graphics Ltd.
Anstey, Leicestershire
Printed and bound in Great Britain by
T. J. International Ltd., Padstow, Cornwall

This book is printed on acid-free paper

The Arrival Of The New

There is something very exciting about the coming of a new year. Ever since I could remember, our family had sat together on the last night of December to celebrate the passing of the old and the arrival of the new.

It was with a sense of awe that we held our vigil on the last night of 1899, for we thought it particularly exhilarating to be entering a new century.

Mam and Dada, born in the 1840s, seemed astonished that we were entering the year 1900 at last.

'There's funny it will be, to be in the nineteen hundreds,' Mam kept saying. 'I never thought to see the day.'

As for the rest of us, we could hardly imagine what the twentieth century might bring!

The five of us were still living at home with our parents, Huw and Susan

Rees, in Cwmbran, a little town in a pleasant Welsh valley.

Dada and my two brothers were miners in the local pit; Gareth was twenty-six and Davey twenty-four. I'm Gwenllian, the middle one — though everyone calls me Gwen. Next came Olwen, at sixteen, and last of all Mari, our little sister, who had just turned ten.

We were settling down after tea when the boys came home, bringing the smell of cold air in with them.

I had cleared away the plates and was about to replace the starched white cloth with the red chenille one, fringed with what Mari called 'the bobbles'.

Dada was sitting in his chair by the fire, attacking his pipe with one of his new pipe cleaners, his Christmas gift from Mari, while Mam was perched on the settle on the opposite side, about to start on the bottomless pile of darning, her usual evening occupation.

'Let it go for once, *cariad*,' Dada told her, but she only smiled and brought out a pullover, frayed at the neck.

There had been a rugby game, with Davey on the team and Gareth as a supporter, and both boys were in good spirits.

'Beat them hollow, we did!' Gareth said, blowing on his cold hands.

'Had your tea, did you?' Mam asked, preparing to struggle to her feet, but Gareth waved her back.

'Ay, there was food in the clubhouse. I could do with a cup of tea, though. How about you, Davey?'

Davey's reply was to shout through to the scullery, where Olwen was clattering the dishes about with bad grace.

'Make us a pot of tea, *fach*, will you?'

'I'll do it,' I said, getting up hastily. The crash of the saucepan on the draining board warned me that Olwen was about to erupt into one of her famous tempers and I was determined that nothing should spoil this special night.

Forbidden by Dada to go down to

the town square with her friends, she was furious at having to wash up the tea things, even though she had missed her turn for the past three evenings.

Mari came running in, throwing her coat down on a chair and earning a frown from Dad, which she cheerfully ignored. He doted on his youngest child and had let her go outside to play after tea, but now she was back inside, eager not to miss anything.

'Not another potato in your stocking, child!' Mam heaved a sigh. 'As if I don't have enough to do without mending them every five minutes!'

Mari went red. The knees and heels of her hated black stockings sprouted holes on a daily basis, and it was only a matter of time before she would be given the task of mending them herself.

But nothing could spoil her joy for long. For the first time in her life, she was being allowed to stay up past midnight and there would be the additional treat of sharing in the metheglin, the lovely homemade honey wine which we always had at New Year.

'Only a sip, mind,' Mam said. 'To toast the new century.'

When we were seated around the table with our cups of tea, we looked at each other expectantly, wondering what to do next. A sing-song would come later, of course, but what to do in the meantime?

Then I had an idea . . .

'When we go back to school, I mean to set my pupils a composition telling about their hopes and dreams for the new century. Let's share our own plans now, shall we?'

'You mean, write an essay?' Mari was horrified. She suffered enough from having her big sister as a teacher at her school, without additional homework tasks on this special night!

'Na, na.' I laughed. 'Just talk, Mari.'

'I shall go on as before.' Mam smiled. 'That will be enough for me.'

Dada gave her an affectionate smile. A happy family life was reward enough for Mam after a lifetime of hard work.

Dad turned to me. 'You next, Gwen.'

'I suppose I'm the same. I like things as they are, living at home and teaching at Cwmbran School. Marriage and children some day, maybe — if anybody asks me.'

Olwen, coming in from the scullery, looked in my direction and curled her lip. I knew what she was thinking; a marvellous new century and here was her dull sister, resisting change as usual.

'I'm going to be a missionary!' Mari announced.

'I thought you wanted to be a teacher?' Dada said. 'Or a nurse. That was what you said last week.'

She nodded importantly.

'Yes, Dada. I could do both. I could teach the heathen and look after them if they were ill.'

'In a leper colony, is it?' David teased, but Gareth said nothing.

My elder brother would have made an excellent medical missionary, but as a miner's son, he couldn't afford the training. Becoming a doctor had been his childhood dream, but at the age of sixteen he had left school and joined Dada in the Cwmbran colliery, where he was likely to remain so long as he had his health and strength.

So he was resigned to his fate, and instead of going to Africa, he served as a lay preacher at the chapel.

Our brother Davey had a different nature altogether. Fiery and full of energy, he was always talking about some cause dear to his heart.

* * *

Now, he and Gareth spoke up for improved working conditions in the mines and for a while the discussion grew quite heated until Mam brought them back down to earth.

'What about you, Olwen? What changes do you see for yourself in the new century?'

Olwen pouted. 'Something a bit more exciting than there is now in this dead and alive hole, I should hope!'

A flash of irritation crossed Dada's face.

'Don't speak to your mam like that, my girl. Only asking a civil question, she is.'

'Never mind, *cariad*, you'll soon see a bit of life when you go to work at Cwmbran House,' said Mam, ever the peacemaker. 'There's a job going there now, I heard. Under-housemaid. Just the thing for you.'

We were all surprised at the vehemence with which Olwen refused to consider it.

'I won't go there, and you can't make me!' she shouted.

'Lower your voice, girl, and don't use that tone with your mam.'

'I don't care. I don't want to be some old skivvy for the Morgans.'

Mam looked hurt. 'I was in service myself before I was married, as well you know, and good, honest work it was, too. And a good preparation for marriage, learning to do things properly around the house.

'The pay isn't much, but you get your meals and lodging, and all the fun of working with other girls your own age.'

Olwen sniffed. 'Fun, is it? I've been talking to Gladys from next door and she says working there is no joke, with that old witch of a housekeeper they have.'

'Oh, you know Gladys!' I put in, trying to lighten the atmosphere. 'Always grumbling about something!'

Gladys Roberts was a kitchen-maid at Cwmbran House, home of the mine owner, Watkin Morgan. She tended to see life in shades of black and white.

'Well, I won't go, and I don't have to. There's a job going at Evans the draper, and Miss Evans says I can have it if I want. I've to let her know tomorrow.'

'And when were you thinking of telling me about this?'

Dada spoke quietly, but the rest of us kept our eyes on the tablecloth, well aware of the calm before the storm.

Dada was normally the kindest of men and slow to anger, but when roused his fury was a sight to behold.

But Olwen would not be stopped.

'I'm telling you now, Dada. And my mind is made up.'

Dada half rose from his chair as Olwen skipped nimbly from the room, taking her coat down from the peg as she went.

'And where do you think you're going, young madam?'

'Out.'

Something in Mam's face made Olwen pause.

'Over to see Bronwen,' she added quickly. 'She wants to show me the material for her new dress.'

Then she flounced out of the house, leaving Mam and Dada to exchange bewildered glances.

'Women!' Davey said, grinning. 'Always wanting to rule the roost. That's one thing that will never change!'

★　★　★

The first day of the new century dawned clear and bright. I was awakened before six o'clock by the singing of small boys who were hoping to collect a *calennig*, or New Year's gift.

'I say one, and you say two,
I say Charlie, how d'you do,
So early in the morning,
So early in the morning,
So early in the morning,
Before the break of day.'

Pulling on my dressing-gown, I hurried downstairs, hoping that Mam's sleep would not be disturbed.

Three urchins stood outside, shivering in the early morning damp.

'*Bore da*, Miss Rees!'

Wishing them good morning in return, I recognised them as three of my former pupils, now in my friend Dilys's class.

One held out his talisman for my inspection — a wizened apple stuck with skewers and decorated with a sprig of mistletoe, a symbol of fruitfulness for the coming year. Strange that in our valley, where the chapel had such influence, this ancient pagan custom had survived so long . . .

I gave them some home-made treacle toffee, and an extra penny apiece for good luck in the new century, and they scampered off gleefully.

Back inside, I tended to the fire, which had been banked down with coal dust for the night, and soon had a good blaze going.

Waiting for the kettle to boil, I looked with affection at the old fireplace, which was truly the heart of the house — a grate and a wide hob, with an oven set in the brick wall. Up above, there was a long mantel, displaying a number of knick-knacks.

Taking pride of place on one end was a small diamond-shaped carving, hard and shiny, chipped out of what we call the black gold, the anthracite coal that provided us all with our living.

I reached for the teapot and took

down the tea caddy with Queen Victoria's picture on it. Mam should have a warming cup in bed, a rare treat for her to bring in the new year . . .

Later that day, I called for Dilys, and we went for a walk around the town.

'Do anything special last night, did you?' I asked.

'Tidied the house and went to bed early.' She pulled a face. 'What did you expect? Cinderella, that's me.'

Dilys kept house for her widowed father, the Methodist minister. There was no dancing in the town square until midnight for her. It was rumoured that when the clock struck twelve, a certain amount of kissing and hugging went on, but as respectable schoolmistresses, that was not for us.

'What about you, Gwen? A cosy evening, I suppose?'

I knew that poor Dilys was envious of our large family, for she was an only child and had a difficult time of it with her withdrawn father. She poured out all her affection on her pupils and was

13

much loved in return.

'Up to a point,' I told her. 'Olwen put a damper on it — as usual. Mam brought up the idea of her taking a job as housemaid at Cwmbran House, and Olwen got quite nasty about it. Thinks herself too good for that — which is an insult to Mam, who was in service herself.'

'What will she do instead, then?'

'Apparently she has the promise of a job at Evans the draper.'

'Nothing wrong with that, is there?'

'Of course not. It's the way she did it, going behind Dada's back, and then giving him cheek. No doubt the fuss will die down in time.'

We strolled in the direction of the shops, through the little park, where children shouted joyously as they bowled their hoops, past the tattered hoarding which warned that 'The wages of sin is death' and on into the high street, with its toy shop, book shop and the milliner's.

We peered through the window of the

draper's shop, catching a glimpse of Gwilym Evans, a little old dormouse of a man, and his spinster sister.

Here, Olwen was destined to toil daily, decently clad in a black frock with a clean white collar and cuffs, measuring out yards of tape and matching samples of yarn for the local housewives. Not the life I would have chosen for myself . . .

In Broad Street, we stopped at the fishmonger's. Dilys went in to buy something for her father's tea while I stayed outside.

'A nice piece of cod, they had,' Dilys said, displaying her damp package. 'I could fancy it fried, but Father always has to have it boiled, with a white sauce. Ugh!'

On we went, past the butcher's shop, and then we sauntered down the hill, towards the recreation ground, where small boys kicked a football about.

'Gwen! See who's coming!'

Recovering from a painful dig in the ribs, I looked up to see our headmaster approaching, actually crossing the street to speak to us, tipping his hat as he came.

'*Bore da*, Miss Parry. *Bore da*, Miss Rees. *Blwyddin newydd da I chwi*.'

Having returned his greetings, we stood awkwardly gazing at each other until he muttered something about seeing us both tomorrow, and marched on his way.

'What was all that about?' I wondered. 'He might as well have called his new year greetings across to us without coming over. The street is narrow enough, heaven knows.'

Dilys took me by the elbow, her face alight with mischief.

'Ah, but he wanted to have a look at Miss Rees close to, didn't he? I saw his face when he looked at you. I think Bryn Edwards is sweet on you, Gwen Rees!'

'Don't be silly, Dilys. Of course he isn't. He wouldn't be interested in me.'

'Don't be too sure.'

My face was flaming, but I was not displeased.

'I wanted him for myself, of course,' Dilys continued. 'But I'd be willing to let my best friend have him.'

'There's silly you are, Dilys.'

'Not at all. Do you want to be an old maid school-teacher all your life? Twenty-two already and not a man in sight.'

'Well, and aren't you the same?' I retorted.

'I'll never marry, Gwen. I can't leave Father. Any husband of mine would have to live with us, and that would never do. You know what Father is like.'

I did indeed. I suppressed a smile at the notion of Reverend Mr Parry and Bryn Edwards under one roof. Better leave Bryn to me, I thought, then laughed at myself for being so silly.

★　★　★

We were back at school for the spring term. A few years earlier I had been a pupil at Cwmbran School myself, but now I was one of the teachers.

I had charge of the infants. Dilys taught those up to the age of ten and old Miss Williams extended her iron control over the older ones up to the age of fourteen.

I had spent several years as a pupil under Miss Williams and had learned to respect her although, like most of her pupils, I was terrified of her at first. She was far too handy with the cane and she had a look in her eye that could quell the antics of the most defiant boy.

When all else failed, she would ask, in a threatening manner, 'Do you want to go to the Meistr?' and of course, nobody did.

The Meistr, of course, was Bryn Edwards, whose methods were quite different from those of Miss Williams. He was a gentle man whose authority stemmed not from the cane, but from his ability to reason with children and make them see the error of their ways.

Besides keeping the school in good

order, he also taught scripture and Welsh history, conducted morning prayers and took the boys for physical training.

As if regretting the impulse that had brought him across the street to speak to us, Bryn behaved coolly, keeping any necessary discussion of school matters to a minimum.

Dilys was wrong, I thought, for as far as I could see he treated us all with the same amount of respect, old Miss Williams included.

Our country abounds in ancient legends and Bryn loved to share these with the children. One Friday afternoon, he came into my classroom and told some of these stories to the little ones, who hung on his every word.

I took as great an interest in those old tales as my pupils did and, of course, Dilys grinned when I mentioned this to her.

'Only interested in his old stories, are you? I see! Are you sure that's all it is, Gwen Rees?'

'Do stop going on about the Meistr, Dilys. Of course I'm not keen on him. What good would that do?'

Although I scolded her, deep down I knew that I was becoming fond of Bryn Edwards, who, apart from anything else, was pleasing to the eye. I felt my heart turn over whenever he smiled at me. But was there any chance for me?

There's silly you are, Gwenllian Rees, I told myself. He's the Meistr and you are just the infants' teacher. Get on with your work and mind your own business!

At night, in the room I shared with my sisters, I peered despairingly at myself in the mirror. Nothing to write home about, I thought with a sigh. Two eyes, a nose, a mouth. It was a pleasant enough face, I supposed, but that was all.

My one beauty was my hair, which was the colour of golden-ripe corn. But it was usually pinned into a respectable bun, as befitted a school-teacher. And when I was at chapel or out in public, it remained hidden under a staid felt hat.

'A handsome man like Bryn wouldn't look twice at someone like me,' I thought dolefully as I brushed my hair.

Bryn Speaks

The weeks passed, taking with them the worst of the winter, and then, wonder of wonders, everything changed. Bryn approached me one night after chapel, asking if he could see me home. My heart thumped painfully. This surely meant something, I thought . . .

I nodded shyly and fell into step beside him. Mam raised her eyebrows and shot a delighted smile in the direction of Dada, who motioned Mari to his side. She would willingly have played gooseberry, I knew! Her big sister having the headmaster as an admirer was something she could use to lord it over her classmates.

I was tongue-tied all the way home, and when Bryn left me at the door of our house, I was sure he wouldn't ask me a second time.

'Goodnight, Miss Rees,' he said

softly. 'Perhaps I can walk again with you next Sunday?'

Awkwardly I mumbled my acceptance and hurried indoors.

In those days, such a relationship was known as 'walking out'. The daughters of people like the Morgans at Cwmbran House took part in parties and balls, and when in London attended plays and the opera, accompanied by suitable young men.

Ordinary people had no such opportunities. There were various societies or choirs that one could join, but they made no provision for sweethearts to be alone.

Country walks were all we needed and, if things became more serious, the young man would be invited home to tea to meet his future in-laws.

The sedate progress of the relationship gave the couple the chance to get to know each other before a commitment was made.

As time went on, I became more and more fond of Bryn, although I wasn't sure if he returned my feelings. We simply enjoyed each other's company, talking of everything and anything on our walks together.

As I have said, he was a handsome man, but there was more to Bryn Edwards than good looks alone. He had an endearing sense of humour and I always knew when some piece of wit was on the tip of his tongue because his mouth began to twitch at the corners and his eyes began to sparkle.

Like a silly schoolgirl, I found myself doodling on scraps of paper when I should have been doing something more constructive, *Gwenllian Edwards, Mrs Bryn Edwards* . . .

At school, of course, Bryn and I were Mr Edwards and Miss Rees, who behaved with the utmost propriety at all times. When he had occasion to come to my classroom to speak to me when the children were out at play, we were careful to leave the door open. We had our reputations to think of and any breath of scandal could have cost us both our jobs.

* * *

The first of March is the day on which Welsh people throughout the world celebrate the feast of their patron saint, Dewi Sant. It was always a special day at Cwmbran School, with singing and storytelling in the morning, and a half-holiday in the afternoon. Girls wore traditional dress, with a daffodil pinned to the breast, while each of the boys sported a leek.

The last days of February were always an anxious time for the girls, as they kept a watchful eye on the sprouting daffodils. Would the flowers open in time, or would they be obliged to make paper ones instead? It was always nicer to have the real thing.

Needless to say, none of us in the miners' cottages had gardens in which to grow daffodils. Our front doors opened on to the street, and most of the small backyards were taken up with a lavatory, wash-house and clothes-line, with possibly a hutch or two for rabbits or pigeons.

On the other hand, the woods which flanked the drive to Cwmbran House were golden with daffodils in season. Kind Mrs Morgan graciously allowed the schoolgirls to go there to pick their St David's Day emblems.

'Just take one or two, mind you,' Bryn cautioned. 'One for yourself and perhaps another for your mam. No sneaking off with great bunches!'

'If you're going to the woods, I'll come with you,' he told me later. 'I could do with some exercise, cooped up here all week.'

So, on that last day of February, we were out in Morgan's woods, in search of flowers.

This would normally have been Mari's treat, but she had a slight cold and Mam had decreed that she must stay in bed or risk missing the celebrations at school the following day.

We parted company at the fork in the path, with Bryn promising to call me if he found anything worth picking. I wandered along, relishing the cool breeze, until I found a patch of buds, still tightly furled. Perhaps if I took some home and stood them in a jug of warm water they might open in time?

As I straightened up with three sturdy stalks in my hand, I caught a glimpse of two figures some way down the ride: a young woman on a horse, accompanied by a man on foot, probably a groom. Miss Verity, I supposed; grown up now and riding a proud bay mare.

It crossed my mind that a groom would hardly be on foot while she rode, but the man might be some estate worker, or even a visitor to the house.

Something about the set of his shoulders and the shape of the head reminded me of our Davey, but of course it couldn't possibly be him — could it?

Before I could get a further glimpse,

the pair disappeared into the trees.

'A penny for them, Gwen?'

I had not heard Bryn coming up behind me, and I jumped.

'Bryn!' I gasped. 'You startled me.'

'No wonder.' He smiled. 'You were miles away.'

I smiled in return.

'I was just thinking,' I said. 'I just caught sight of the young lady of the house, Miss Verity, on her horse.'

'Nothing strange about that, *fach*. Home from London, they say. If I had a grand house and acres of land and a thoroughbred horse to ride on, I'd be out surveying my kingdom, too.'

'But there was a man with her. On foot,' I told him. 'From a distance, I could have sworn it was our Davey.'

'Hardly likely, is it? One of her grand friends from London, I'd say.'

'I'm sure you're right,' I said, though, really, I doubted the words even as I said them.

★ ★ ★

Mari received her daffodil with a pout. Mam, taking it from her, said, 'Don't worry, *cariad*. With any luck, it will open up overnight. We'll leave it by the warmth of the stove, see.'

I spent the evening getting ready for the great day. Shawls and aprons had to be found, and the traditional Welsh headgear retrieved from the hat box on top of Mam's wardrobe.

Having heated the goffering iron on the fire, I tackled the fluted edging on the white caps which were worn under the hats.

Lastly, the tall black hats were given a good brushing. Some of the girls possessed fine beaver hats — family heirlooms made from furs which had come from Canada. Alas, ours were poor imitations, made of stiff felt, but at least we looked the part.

We set off in the morning, careful to hold on to our hats. For once, Mari deigned to walk with me; usually she scorned to be seen walking with the teacher, even if I was her own sister.

When we reached the school, she ran off to the entrance reserved for 'the big girls', and I went on to my own classroom.

Soon the bell rang and the children marched into the room, bid me good morning and sat down.

The partition between the other two classrooms was removed and a monitor summoned us in.

The children almost lifted the roof with their singing. We worked our way through all the traditional songs like '*Sosban Fach*', '*Migaldia Magaldi*' and '*Men of Harlech*'.

Mrs Morgan gave a performance on her harp, playing some lively tunes. Then she stood up to speak, receiving a great cheer when she announced the expected half-holiday.

I looked at her thoughtfully. Seeing Mrs Morgan brought home the scene in the woods. The more I thought about it, the more I was sure that the man had been our Davey.

There was a great gulf between the

family of the mine owner and his employees. Any friendship between Miss Verity and one of the miners could only lead to trouble for all concerned.

As I walked home that day I was greatly troubled . . .

★　★　★

The summer came, with four weeks off from school, to the delight of pupils and teachers alike.

Mari brought home a good report, which was received with pride by Mam and Dada, but caused her considerable worry.

'Ceri Davies says I only came top because I'm the teacher's pet,' she said, blinking back tears.

'He's a very naughty boy, then,' Mam consoled. 'Don't you listen to such nonsense. Miss Williams may be strict, but she is fair.'

'But, Mam, Ceri says it's because the Meistr is sweet on our Gwen.'

'That's enough, Mari Rees,' Mam

told her, glancing over at me. 'Out with you now, into the fresh air.'

I spent much of my vacation helping Mam, who had never known what it was to have a holiday. Keeping the family clean and decent in a coal-mining valley was like fighting a losing battle.

I have read novels in which house-wives seem to spend all their time whitening the doorsteps and washing and ironing their net curtains, but their toil must be nothing compared with that of a miner's wife.

Every day, water had to be carried in and heated up to fill the old tin tub in front of the fire, so that Dada and the boys could wash when they came home from the pit. No wonder the boys had so much to say about a dream of pit-head baths!

No once-a-week bath for them like the farm labourers; our men came home with only the whites of their eyes showing in their coal-blacked faces.

Then there was the washing, which

involved boiling clothes in a large pot or scrubbing them on a wash-board, then threading them through the mangle and taking dripping mounds of garments out to the clothes-line.

'There's glad I am to have your help, Gwen,' Mam told me, after I'd dashed outside to rescue sheets from the line in a sudden shower.

She hauled on the pulley to send the clothes rack up to the ceiling and the sheets hung there, steaming, while drops of water sent the fire spitting and hissing down below.

Coming in one evening with an armful of damp shirts ready for ironing, I was surprised to hear raised voices — Dada's loudest of all. He had never before been known to shout, preferring to control his children by the use of a fierce expression which, as Davey often said by way of a joke, could stop a charging bull at fifty paces.

On this occasion, he was reading the riot act while Gareth and Davey glared at him across the table.

'There's foolish, it is, to talk of giving up your good jobs to go to Canada. Different it might be if you were out of work!' He jabbed the stem of his pipe in their direction, his eyes flashing.

'Now, Huw, nobody said they were actually going anywhere,' Mam soothed. 'Just talk, it is. Sit down by the fire and warm yourself and let the boys have their say. There's no harm in dreaming, see. Put the kettle on, Gwen, and we'll have a cup of tea.'

Reluctantly Dada moved back in his chair and my brothers sat down, too, their arms still folded. I moved the kettle over to the hob and looked from one to the other.

'What's going on?' I asked.

'If you read 'The Echo' you'd know,' Gareth said. 'There's been a lot of talk lately about getting Welshmen to go out to Canada to farm. They're opening up land in the West, and there are hundreds of acres free for the taking.

'David Lloyd George is head of a committee that has been touring the area and he says it's just the thing for any man who is willing to work. There are several accounts of Welsh families who've been there for some time, all doing well.'

'Such as that man in Manitoba who went there with a pocketful of money to begin with?' Dada asked. 'Ten thousand pounds, I believe. He has quite a different opinion on the subject.'

He leaned over and searched through a copy of the paper while we waited in silence.

'Here it is. *'Anyone would be insane to think of settling in Canada,'* he says. *'The climate is terrible, freezing in winter and scorching in summer; prices are appalling, and the task of clearing the land is worse than the labours of Hercules'.'*

'Yes, Dada,' Davey said, trying to control his frustration. 'And it also says that he was a disgruntled emigrant who had recently been sacked from his job with the Canadian post office!

'Just think of it, if we went to the West we'd be given a hundred and sixty acres of land apiece, for just a small registration fee, and with the chance to buy more later.' His eyes shone. 'Why, that's more than any of the tenant farmers here will ever see!'

'But the West!' Mam put in. 'Isn't that where all the Indians are? Where they scalp the settlers and burn their houses down?'

'Na, na.' Davey smiled. 'That was the American West, and long ago, too, Mam. Don't worry — Canada is safe as houses.'

Dada accepted his cup of tea and a freshly-baked Welsh cake. Never one to bear a grudge, he had calmed down, and changed the subject by asking me about my day.

★   ★   ★

Later, when the boys had gone to bed, I sat quietly by the fire and listened as Mam and Dada chatted together. It was

Mam who brought up the subject again.

'There's awful, it is, to think of the boys going so far away, Huw. Yet I wonder, is it selfish to want to keep them safe at home, when they could go to Canada and be big farmers?'

'Big fools, more like,' Dada replied. 'This is nothing new, the Welsh going to Canada. Been going in droves for years, they have, and to America, too. Not so bad if they have jobs to go to, but this farming business is a different thing. They have no farming experience and no capital. How would they buy the livestock they need to set themselves up? Na, *cariad*, let the cobbler stick to his last, I say.'

A day or two later, I recounted this conversation to Bryn.

'I remember reading about gentlemen farmers who went to Canada after the war with Napoleon,' he said, 'when land was being given out in the Eastern provinces. They were usually discharged soldiers, and the younger sons of

English landowners.

'Many of them expected their new land to be much like their own family estates, where the owners live off the rents paid by their tenants. What they received were vast tracts of virgin forest, which had to be cleared before crops could be planted. You can imagine how appalled they were to learn they had to perform the labour themselves. They weren't used to working with their hands, see.'

'But if it was all so difficult, I wonder why all those Irish and Scots were so glad to go there?' I mused, recalling what Dada, a great reader of history, had told me.

'Better that than starve.'

A sad look came over Bryn's face. I knew he was remembering his Irish grandmother, who had come to Wales as a child with what was left of her family to escape the potato famine. He had grown up with those tales of grief and privation.

Now my own brothers wanted to go

to the Canadian West, where they, too, would have to clear the land and struggle to survive. Well, they were no strangers to hard work, and possibly they longed to live in the fresh air rather than toiling like moles far below the ground. I could hardly blame them for that.

In the days that followed, the atmosphere in our little house became more strained. Mam went about her work tight-lipped.

The boys spent most of their free time in their room, where the murmur of their voices floated through to the kitchen. I longed to shout at them, begging them not to go, but daren't say a word. Davey was stubborn as a mule, and any interference could push him in the wrong direction. Like Mam, I could only hope they would see sense.

Finally, Dada could stand it no longer.

'You are grown men and you have the right to choose. Go if you must, with my blessing.'

Mam's eyes were full of tears, but she managed to smile.

Gareth and Davey slapped each other on the back. 'Canada, here we come!'

Great Expectations

The weeks flew by and, almost before I knew it, we were approaching the first Christmas of the new century. Bryn and I had been walking out together for almost a year and I had high hopes that something might soon be said about a more permanent arrangement.

Mam and Dada approved of Bryn as a possible son-in-law and he got on well with the rest of the family, so there was nothing to stand in our way.

One afternoon, I was busy in my classroom, helping my pupils make Christmas decorations. The desks were covered in strips of gaily-coloured paper, which the children were making into chains, and two of the older boys were mixing up a fresh batch of flour and water paste.

'Please, Miss, Ceinwen Pugh put glue on my hair!' a young voice wailed.

I was busy attending to the sticky problem when the door opened. It was Bryn, nodding and smiling as the children held up their work for his inspection.

'I can see you're busy, Miss Rees,' he said. 'Can you stay behind after school? I have something for you.'

I nodded, trying to keep from smiling. 'I was going to stay behind, anyway. I want to check the costumes for the nativity play.'

Bryn left, leaving me all of a-twitter, as Mam would say. The costumes didn't need checking at all! Most of the children would be dressed as shepherds, wearing dressing-gowns with tea towels on their heads.

Several beautifully-carved shepherds' crooks stood in a corner. They were the real thing, belonging to some of the fathers who worked as shepherds. Besides the coal mine, which employed so many of the local men, Cwmbran was also sheep-farming country.

When the last of the children had

gone away, chattering happily, I tried to tidy myself for Bryn's return. Sure that I was about to receive a proposal, I wished I'd worn something prettier to school. However, there was nothing I could do about it now!

The glass on the picture of the young Queen Victoria gave back a dull reflection as I made an attempt to control my hair, which was escaping from its pins. When I caught a movement in my make-shift mirror, I turned and saw Bryn. He was holding out a small box.

'This is for you.' He beamed happily at me.

I took it with trembling hands. Not much of a proposal, I thought, but I knew by now that Bryn was a rather shy man. Besides, what did words matter between two people in love?

The box sprang open and there, resting on a bed of blue velvet, was a small brooch. It was enamelled in blue with the word Mizpah picked out in gold.

Not a ring after all. My face felt

frozen as I tried to smile.

'Do you like it, Gwen?' Bryn asked, still beaming. 'It belonged to my mother. My father gave it to her when I was born.'

Somehow, I managed to say all the right things until finally he had gone, saying that he would see me in the morning.

I snatched up my bag and rushed out of the school.

I don't know how I got home. I certainly don't recall passing the familiar landmarks. When I burst into the house, Mam took one look at my face and made me sit down.

'What's wrong, *cariad*?' she asked gently. 'Did something happen up the school?'

I took out the little box and thrust it across the table. Mam opened it wonderingly, and her face lit up when she saw the brooch.

'A Mizpah brooch! There's lovely!' she exclaimed. 'I haven't seen one of these for years.'

'Bryn gave it to me for Christmas. It belonged to his mother.'

'And you were hoping for an engagement ring, is that it?' She looked at me, her eyes bright.

'We've been keeping company for months, Mam! I thought he'd have made up his mind by now, and then to give me an old brooch! I don't even know what Mizpah means.'

'It's from the Scriptures, *fach*. And Mizpah . . . 'the Lord watch between me and thee when we are absent from one another.' It's a lovely thought. And to give you his mother's brooch, too! He must think highly of you.'

'Not enough to marry me, it seems.'

'Give him time, *cariad*, give him time,' Mam soothed. 'No good rushing into marriage.'

'But I'm almost twenty-three, Mam. Olwen already laughs at me for being an old maid.'

'Too flighty by half is our Olwen.' Mam smiled. 'Your time will come, Gwenllian. Have patience and you'll see.'

I nodded slowly, understanding the sense in her words. But still, deep in my heart, I knew there was something holding Bryn back. He wasn't ready to settle down, I feared. And, more importantly, he wasn't ready to settle down with me . . .

★　★　★

I was washing my hair when Megan Roberts called round from next door. I was rather surprised when she invited me to tea on Sunday afternoon. I had never been particularly close to Megan — she was older than me — but our Gareth and her brother, Llew, had been friends since their school days and now worked the same shift at the mine.

'It's our Glad's afternoon off,' she told me, 'and she's coming home. I thought I'd invite a few people in. You know how Mamgu loves a bit of gossip and I hear there's a bit of trouble at the House. Miss Verity as usual!'

Of course I was interested to hear

that. I might learn more about what I was beginning to believe was Davey's 'involvement' with that young woman!

'I'd love to — only I promised Dilys I'd spend the afternoon with her. She doesn't get out much, thanks to the Reverend Mr Parry being so demanding.'

'Oh, Dilys can come, too,' Megan told me. 'Only a cup of tea, it is, and a bit of cake. One more won't make much difference. You must come, Gwen; our Llew would be glad to see you.'

The last thing I needed was Llew Roberts making sheep's eyes at me. Then I thought, if Bryn got wind of someone else looking in my direction, it might give him a nudge.

The Roberts family had turned their front room into living quarters for Mamgu, their grandmother. When we were very young, Mr and Mrs Roberts had both died, leaving their children, Llew, Gladys and Megan, to Mamgu's care.

Now Mamgu was bedridden and spent her days and nights in an iron bed beside the front window, where she could keep an eye on the outside world. In the good weather, the window was left open and friends passing by could stop to have a word with her. She loved to catch up on all the local news.

Dilys was agog to hear my worries about Davey and Miss Verity. Like Bryn, she had been sceptical at first. But then she decided it was romantic; the heiress and the miner, like something out of a penny novelette.

'Not so romantic if it's true and Mr Morgan finds out!' I pointed out. 'We could all end up in the poorhouse if Davey gets the sack — and maybe Gareth and Dada, too!'

* * *

Later, we all gathered in the Roberts' front room to hear what Gladys had to say. Mamgu sat bright-eyed on her bed, while the rest of us perched on kitchen chairs, dressed in our Sunday best.

'Come on then, *fach*, tell us about Miss Verity,' Megan urged.

'Well, the Morgans are trying to arrange a marriage for her, and she'll have none of it.'

'Listening at doors, was you, our Gladys?' Mamgu asked, a mischievous glint in her eye.

'Na, na, Mamgu!' Gladys protested. 'It was Mrs Morgan's ladies' maid, Miss Richards, she heard it first. She told the housekeeper, who told Cook. She was doing Mrs Morgan's hair when Mr Morgan came in and started to talk — and you know how they think servants are too deaf or too stupid to understand.'

'Well, get on with it, girl! Why would they want to arrange a marriage for Miss Verity? A pretty young lady like her, due to come into money in time — why, the lads must be lined up six deep.'

Gladys held out her cup to Megan, who silently refilled it.

'According to Cook, if a girl don't get spoken for by the end of the season, it's a disgrace,' said Gladys. 'And there was no proposal for Miss Verity. Mind you, they say she did nothing in London to help herself. Went around with her eyes lowered and wouldn't speak up. Men like a bit of life in a girl, see?

'Home she came last spring in floods of tears, as I know for a fact. She was moping about the house like a lost soul.'

I caught my breath. It was last spring I had seen Verity in the wood with Davey!

'I heard her tell Miss Richards she'd never marry now,' Gladys continued. 'And Miss Richards said, 'There, there, of course you will,' and Miss Verity said she wanted to be a nun instead.

'The next thing was, they packed her off back to London, to stay with her Auntie Clarissa. More eligible men up in London, you see.'

'Thought you had something interesting to tell us, I did.' Mamgu looked disappointed. 'Nothing new about a girl left on the shelf. Look at our Megan — and Miss Dilys Parry, too.'

Megan's fists clenched. She'd been engaged to be married for more than two years, but couldn't leave Mamgu. Her future husband would not move into the house with them, insisting he wanted to set up their own home elsewhere. Megan had told Mam that she was waiting for Llew to marry and bring a wife into the house, and then she would be off like lightning.

As for Dilys, it was a sore point with her that she was still unattached at the age of twenty-three.

'That's where you're wrong, then,' Gladys went on. 'Miss Verity did meet someone, but he turned out to be a rotter! Paid her a lot of attention and even proposed — but he was only after her money.'

Mamgu leaned forward, dismayed. 'There's terrible!' she exclaimed. 'What will the poor girl do now?'

'Mr Morgan says he'll arrange her

marriage to some reliable man and hear no more nonsense.'

The door opened then, and Gareth and Llew joined us. The talk turned to other things, but I sat in silence for a while.

I felt some sympathy for Miss Verity, but I hoped her father would arrange for her to be married to someone of her own class, and soon. Then Davey would be safe . . .

Soon, Dilys had to leave to help her father get ready for the evening service. As we stood outside, she turned to me.

'He's rather nice, isn't he?' she whispered.

'Who is?' I asked stupidly.

'Why, Llew, of course. Really, Gwen, where have you been all afternoon? Off in the clouds, is it, with your mind on the Meistr?'

'Something like that,' I murmured, and she waved goodbye.

'I like your friend, Dilys, Gwen,' Gareth told me as we headed for home. 'I wouldn't mind getting to know her better. Would she go out with me if I asked her?'

I smiled. 'You won't know until you do.'

'Ah, but that's where you come in,' he said, nudging me playfully. 'Put in a good word for me, will you, *fach*?'

★　★　★

The news came on a wet day in January. I was in the classroom, trying to drum the words of a psalm into the heads of my pupils. The children had just faltered to a halt and I'd asked them to begin again when Bryn came in.

'I have some bad news,' he said. 'Her Majesty Queen Victoria is dead. She passed away on the twenty-first of January.'

I was shocked. The Queen had been very old but she'd come to the throne when my grandparents were children. Few people in the vast empire would ever have imagined life without her.

One of the boys put up his hand. 'What will happen, Sir?' he asked. 'Who will be queen now?'

'We'll have a king, Ceri. The Prince of Wales will now come to the throne as King Edward the Seventh.'

There was a stir of excitement. The Prince of Wales!

'The Prince of Wales is the title given to the eldest son of the monarch, but he is not a Welsh prince,' Bryn explained, reading their minds.

'Now,' he continued, 'when you go home I want each of you to ask your mother to make you a black armband. We must wear it in mourning for the Queen.'

After this excitement, the children were too worked up to continue learning their Bible verses. I told them they could each draw a picture of the Prince of Wales and the best efforts would be pinned up on the wall.

I wondered what sort of king he would make. He had waited such a long time to come to the throne, and if the newspaper stories were to be believed, his mother had not allowed him any involvement in affairs of state. He had spent his days in pleasurable pursuits.

When I got home, Mam had heard the news and was dabbing at her eyes with the corner of her apron.

'Not long since she had her diamond jubilee, and now she's gone to glory, poor thing.'

'She was very old, Mam.'

At that moment Olwen returned, banging the door behind her. Her eyes were red and swollen — she had obviously been crying.

'Olwen, *cariad*, whatever is the matter?' Mam wanted to know at once.

'Only lost my job, haven't I?' Olwen wailed, searching for her handkerchief once more.

'What did you do?' Mari asked.

'Why does everyone always assume I'm to blame?' Olwen snapped. 'I haven't done anything wrong. It's Mr Evans — he's dead. I found out when I went to work this morning.'

'Oh, the poor man,' Mam put in. 'My, but it's a day of bad news. First the Queen, and now this. But surely Mr Evans' sister will keep the shop going?'

Olwen shook her head sadly.

'No, Mam. She's going to live with her sister, who keeps a guesthouse at the Mumbles. The shop goes to their nephew. It was all arranged some time ago.

'Miss Evans told me they have three daughters who all want to come into the shop, so they won't need me. I've been given a month's notice.'

'It never rains but it pours,' Mam muttered, but Mari had the last word.

'You'll have to go to work at Cwmbran House now,' she piped up.

Olwen gave her a furious look before rushing out of the room.

★ ★ ★

The days grew milder and the evenings lighter as the weeks went by. Olwen worked out her notice in a rather sullen

56

fashion, only pulling herself together when Dada lost patience with her.

'You keep this up, my girl, and you won't be getting a good reference. Then where will you be?'

Gareth plucked up the courage to ask Dilys out. She accepted, although she still made pointed references to Llew Roberts whenever we got together. However, when Llew made no move in her direction, she invited Gareth home for tea.

Her father approved of Gareth. My brother was a pillar of the chapel, and they spent all one teatime discussing a forthcoming sermon — much to Dilys's chagrin.

'Your Gareth was supposed to be visiting me,' she complained. 'Not sitting there like a stuffed dummy, thinking of suitable texts for Father!'

And I had problems of my own . . .

One Sunday afternoon, I went walking in Morgan's wood, and saw Davey again. I was by myself because Bryn was busy, so I decided it was time to get to the bottom of the mystery. He was a hundred yards ahead of me and I quickened my pace.

'Davey!' I called, and he turned to face me.

'Where are you going?' I gasped as I reached him.

'None of your business!' he growled, but I wasn't going to let him get away with that.

We stood there, glowering at each other. It wasn't a good combination. I'd always been impulsive and prone to blurting things out; and Davey was always stubborn, never willing to give in.

'Going to see Verity Morgan, are you?' I demanded.

'What makes you think that?' He was blushing.

'I saw you together, months ago, walking down this very path.'

'Spying on me, then?'

'I was not. I happened to be here gathering daffodils for Dewi Sant, and there you were, in plain sight.'

He gave a sigh, and I knew I had won.

'Oh, Davey, what on earth is the matter with you? Can't you find a nice girl from the chapel? What can you possibly have in common with Watkin Morgan's daughter?'

'The Morgans are no better than us,' he growled.

'Not better, Davey — just different, that's all. Verity's had so many advantages; she's been educated, she's used to servants. You're a miner living in a two-up, two-down house, with no prospects.'

He didn't reply and I pressed on. 'How did all this get started?'

'It was the day you saw us together,' he muttered. 'I'd come for a walk in the fresh air; I need it, working below ground in the pit all week. I found Verity lying on the ground, stunned. Her horse had thrown her. What was I supposed to do? Leave the girl lying there?

'I helped her back to the house and

on the way we talked a bit. After that, we met once or twice, but then she went back to London. I thought that was the end of it — until she began to write to me.'

'But no letters came to the house . . .'

'Gladys,' he volunteered before I could ask.

I saw it all now. Poor, foolish Gladys, with her head filled with romantic notions, had been a willing participant in this silly affair, giving no thought to the consequences of her actions — or theirs!

'Oh, Davey!' I sighed. 'What will you do?'

'Don't you worry yourself, *fach*.' Davey's eyes were gazing past me to some far-off horizon. 'Everything will work out somehow. And you can be sure that Verity'll not marry the man her father's found for her. He's fifty if he's a day!'

I shook my head sadly. What would become of my brother now?

He patted my arm. 'Now, go home, Gwen,' he said quietly. 'And, please, not a word of this — not to anyone.'

* * *

Surprisingly, nothing happened in the next few days. I was just beginning to hope that I had made my brother see sense when Megan came to the house.

'I'm here to ask a favour, Gwen,' she said. 'Could you come in tonight and sit with Mamgu while I go out for a bit to see Gwilym? She's not been well and I don't want to leave her alone, but if I don't get away for an hour, I think I'll burst.' She sighed. 'She's my grandmother and I love her dearly, but she drives me mad at times.'

'Of course I'll come. You go off and enjoy yourself.'

And, so, there I was, next door, sitting in the lamplight, preparing lessons for school, while Mamgu dozed nearby.

The houses on Jenner Road are

joined together in a long row, so everyone shares a wall with neighbours. On the other side of the wall, beside the chair where I was sitting, was the room where Gareth and Davey slept.

Almost lulled to sleep by Mamgu's snores, I was suddenly jerked to my senses by the sound of an anguished cry from next door.

I rushed back home as fast as I could. When I got in, Mam was rocking back and forth on a kitchen chair, her head in her hands.

'Mam! What's wrong?' The sirens hadn't gone, so it couldn't be an accident at the pit.

'Just went into the boys' room, I did, to put a pig in the bed, it being so damp out tonight. I found that note.'

The stone hot-water bottle was on the table, with a crumpled sheet of paper beside it. I read the few words with growing disbelief.

Dear Mam and Dada,

We have gone to Canada. We thought it best.

Love, Davey.

I had to sit down.

'Nothing more have they said about going to Canada for months now,' Mam was saying. 'I was hoping they'd had second thoughts. And if they had to go, why sneak away in the middle of the night like thieves?

'Dada gave his blessing, they knew that. We would have given them a proper send-off.'

'Perhaps it will turn out all right,' I murmured, but she was not to be comforted.

When Dada came home, he had to be told. Then Mari came in from play and pestered us with so many questions that she was sent to bed, protesting all the way up the stairs.

Olwen came in soon after and, sensing tension, made a cup of cocoa and took it upstairs with her.

I stayed where I was, although there was nothing I could do or say to improve the situation.

Mam sat staring into the fire,

white-faced. Dada sat beside her with an arm round her shoulders, too agitated to settle to anything else. My heart was heavy, but there was nothing I could do or say to comfort my parents.

The clock struck ten and I got up to go to bed, knowing I had to be fresh for school in the morning. That was when the door opened and Gareth came into the room.

'Gareth, *cariad*!' Mam struggled to her feet, her eyes alight with joy.

'We thought you'd gone to Canada, boyo!' Dada exclaimed, jubilant that he hadn't lost both of his sons.

But there was no smile on Gareth's face.

'It's Davey who's gone,' he said. 'He's on his way to Liverpool to catch the boat.'

'But the letter says 'we'.' Mam picked up the note. 'We thought that meant the two of you. What does he mean? Did you change your mind?'

'There were two that went,' Gareth

told us. 'I went after them to the station, to try to talk sense into them, but it was no good. They wouldn't listen. They caught the train and left me standing there.'

'Who, Gareth?' Dada's voice was low.

'Davey has gone to Canada with Verity Morgan.'

Blame For Gareth

Davey's departure affected us all in different ways. Gareth bore the brunt of our father's displeasure, being accused of knowing about the elopement.

'I swear to you, Dada, I knew nothing until the last moment,' Gareth told him.

'Nonsense. You two were close; you shared a room. How could you not know what was going on?'

'I tell you, I knew nothing until I came home and found him packing to go away. I asked him where he was going and he told me then that he was leaving for Canada, and taking Verity Morgan with him.'

'Then you should have come to me!' Dada reasoned. 'Together we might have put a stop to it.'

'I didn't want to worry you.' Gareth gently put his hand on Dada's shoulder.

'I thought I could handle it myself. That's why I followed them to the station, hoping to persuade the girl to see sense. But neither of them would even speak to me.'

'I thought Davey had gone quiet these past few weeks,' Mam put in. 'Hoping, I was, that the pair of you had given up on the idea of going to Canada — especially you, Gareth, now you have a nice young lady to keep you here in Wales.'

'It's nothing to do with Dilys.' Gareth smiled wryly.

I was puzzled by this. Gareth had been fond of our old friend for some time, and I suspected he harboured secret hopes of marrying her one day.

'I was all for going to Canada myself,' Gareth continued. 'It was Davey who went cold on the idea.'

'And now we know why.' Dada was pacing the floor now, like some caged beast in the zoological gardens. 'Verity Morgan, of all people. Old man Morgan will go mad when he finds out.

'It won't surprise me if Gareth and I lose our jobs. Then the lot of us will be out on the streets.'

Mam began to cry softly.

I turned my head away and stared into the fire. As if the solution to our dilemma could be found in the leaping flames!

Were Davey and Verity really in love? All Davey had said was that her father planned to marry her off to some old man. Surely she could have said no and that would have been the end of it? Now her problems had rebounded on us all . . .

* * *

Cwmbran House, where the Morgans lived, was a lovely old place, set in pleasant grounds and surrounded by many acres of agricultural land. Most of the land was farmed by families whose tenancy depended on whether they could pay their rent and, equally important, whether they could keep the goodwill of their landlord.

The miners, too, were utterly dependent on the Morgan family. Not many years before, there had been a strike and Mr Morgan had adopted a hard line, which had persisted after everything returned to normal. He could afford to hold out almost indefinitely, where the miners could not.

I could still remember the worry on Dada's face as he'd watched his meagre savings dwindle. And Mam had seemed to get thinner and thinner as she'd tried to make each penny do the work of two.

We were all aware that any dissidents would soon be given their marching orders, and this worried Mam. Many a night, the talk round the kitchen table concerned working conditions in the mine and the need for change. Hot-headed Davey had been the most outspoken of all.

'Just don't voice your opinions outside this house, boyo,' I remembered Dad advising him. 'It's not just you to consider, but the whole family. Remember your mother and sisters before you speak out of turn.'

Now Davey had done something much worse — and I wondered how long it would be before we were all made to pay for my brother's folly.

I couldn't help thinking that I was somehow to blame for our situation. If only I'd spoken out when I'd first seen Davey with Verity in Morgan's Wood, perhaps things would be different . . .

'Poor Gwen, this is worrying you, isn't it?' Dada's voice disturbed my reverie. 'Never mind, we'll get through it somehow, if we all pull together.'

I managed a weak smile. If only you knew, I thought sadly, turning back to the fire.

⋆   ⋆   ⋆

'What's the matter with Gareth?' Dilys asked a few days later as we stood in the playground, waiting for the children to form lines. 'He was supposed to come round for his tea yesterday and he didn't turn up. Father was so cross. First of all because I served shepherd's pie, and secondly because I waited half an hour to dish up, which put him in a fury.

'"You know I detest made-up dishes,' Father said. Of course, it was either that or eat the rest of the joint cold.

'Then he kept on about how rude Gareth was and perhaps not the man for me after all. Not the man for *him*, he meant. If ever I marry, we'll have to live with Father and he'll expect to be catered to first, ahead of any husband I might bring home.'

'I'm sorry,' I said. 'Gareth has something on his mind.'

Dilys looked at me curiously, but my class had already started to move inside.

'Tell you later,' I called back over my shoulder as I made for the side door behind my pupils.

However, when playtime came and we were able to snatch a quick cup of tea, I found that I dared not tell her the whole story. Fortunately, the news that Davey had gone off to Canada without a word of goodbye satisfied my friend.

'Oh, poor Gareth! No wonder he forgot to come round,' Dilys gushed. 'To think of Davey going without him when they had such big plans to go together.'

She considered this for a while and then brightened up.

'Oh, well, at least this will be a point in Gareth's favour where Father is concerned. It doesn't matter what he thinks of Davey, does it?'

I bridled at that. Davey was my brother, although I knew quite well why Dilys's father, the Reverend Mr Parry, disliked him. He was not the most regular attendant at chapel and once, when he was a good deal younger, had demanded to know why the chapel only had an old tin roof while the church had fine slates and a bell tower.

' 'Lay not up for yourselves treasures on earth, where moth and dust doth corrupt',' Mr Parry had said, which was no answer at all as far as my brother was concerned. The storm in Davey's eyes must have rankled with the fiery minister.

As it happened, Gareth was saved from facing the wrath of Dilys's father by a nasty dose of bronchitis which kept him in bed.

Every time one of her menfolk coughed, Mam started worrying about the dreaded lung diseases which could affect men who worked too long underground. Despite the cost, she always called the doctor at the first sign of trouble.

On this occasion, Dr Murphy prescribed some foul-tasting medicine and handed Gareth a chit for the shift foreman, which Dada could deliver. There would be no pay for the lost days, but his place on the job was safe, at least for the time being.

Dada caught a cold, but insisted on

going to work as usual. Mam was determined that it should not 'go down' as she put it, as it had with Gareth.

When Dada took his nightly bath, there was a good handful of mustard added to the water, while Gareth wore red flannel on his chest, liberally smeared with goose grease, and was made to inhale steam laced with Friar's Balsam.

'And I shall hang a raw onion in the kitchen,' Mam told the unhappy pair. 'I have heard that it will attract the germs to itself and keep them away from people.'

'There's wonderful this house will smell.' Gareth grinned, but he was taken with a fit of coughing until Mam told him to be quiet and behave himself.

So it was that I went alone to chapel on Sunday evening. When I came out into the open air, Llew, our neighbour, joined me on the path and made some comment about the weather. Dilys came hurrying up, followed by Bryn.

'Well, Gwen, shall we be going?' Bryn pulled the watch out of his waistcoat pocket and checked the time. 'I mustn't be out late. I've a mountain of forms to fill out for the office.'

'Oh, I can see Gwen home,' Llew put in. 'I am going the same way, as you know.'

Bryn frowned. He had let himself in for that, sounding as if he grudged the time it would take to go to Jenner Road and back, and Llew lived right next door to me, after all.

'Is that all right with you, Gwen?' Bryn asked, looking hopeful that I would say no.

I smiled. 'Well, you did ask me first, Bryn.'

I was laughing inside, seeing Bryn and Llew eyeing each other up and down, like two dogs spoiling for a fight. Perhaps Bryn would sit up and take more notice now, I thought.

But I also wanted to tell him about Davey and Verity. He would have a sensible opinion, I knew.

'I can hardly believe it, Gwen!' Bryn exclaimed when I'd told him all. 'Davey is an impulsive one, and I had heard that Miss Morgan was wilful . . . But to leave — and to Canada!

'Your father must be so worried — all of you must be worried. What do you make of it all?' Bryn turned and considered me intently.

I shrugged. 'What can I think?' I said, close to tears now at Bryn's kindness and obvious concern. 'I feel I am to blame. After all, I knew what was happening — I could have stopped it.'

'No, Gwen.' His voice was stern now. 'You are not to blame. You could not have known how selfishly they would behave.'

Bryn took hold of my hand, squeezing it gently. 'I'm sure it will all work itself out,' he said. 'Be patient, Gwen.'

I nodded and whispered a goodnight, before hurrying indoors and up to my room.

'Be patient,' Bryn had said. But the tone of his voice — so deliberate and slow — told me there was a deeper meaning in his words . . .

★ ★ ★

A nasty smell of burning greeted me when I got home from school the next day. Mam was beside herself with frustration.

'Look at my *tatws*, all burned to a coal.' She scowled. 'Now what am I going to give your father for his tea?'

I peered into the pot and, sure enough, the potatoes were beyond saving.

'There's lucky it is the bottom is still in the *sosban*,' I remarked. 'I saw the cockle women when I was coming up the road; they'll be here in a minute. Shall I run out and get some?'

'Dada does love a nice feast of cockles, and the cold lamb will keep till tomorrow. Off with you then. Take the white basin and a sixpence from my purse.'

Sure enough, one of the cockle women was just coming into sight, riding a plodding donkey. Wearing rubber boots and a frayed shawl, she dipped into one of the panniers strapped to the beast's side and brought out a scoop of cockles.

The cockle women led a cold, hard life, harvesting the cockles out of the sands of some beach on the South Wales coast.

I wondered how they managed to travel so far inland to sell their wares. Surely they didn't come all those miles on a donkey?

Mam had calmed down somewhat when I went back indoors with my basin of cockles. She had put the pot to soak in the hope of later scouring it back to normal.

'How did it happen, Mam?' I asked. 'It's not like you to take your eyes off the hob.'

'Oh, it's that Olwen.' Mam sighed. 'How she does drive me wild. Arguing with her, I was, and you would not believe the back answers. Ran up the stairs shouting, she did. She'll do that once too often!

'Go and bring her down by here,

cariad, and we'll start again.'

Olwen was in our room, lying on my bed with her dirty shoes on.

'Mam wants you downstairs, Olwen,' I told her. 'And you'd better take your feet off my clean *gwrthban*.'

'Yes, Miss!' she sneered, wrinkling my bed cover as she got to her feet, but taking her time over it.

'What's this all about, Olwen? And shouldn't you be helping Mam, now you're at home with no job?'

'I scraped the potatoes and dusted all round,' Olwen said indignantly. 'But all Mam wants to talk about is me going into service at Cwmbran House. I've told them and told them I won't go skivvying for the Morgans. I did have a good job at the drapers, but only for old Mr Evans dying and putting me out of work.'

Downstairs, Olwen's eyes lit up at the sight of the cockles, but she soon turned sullen again when Mam started to speak.

'You'll do as you are told, my girl,

and go up there in the morning and ask to speak to the housekeeper,' Mam told her. 'You don't have to work there for ever, if it's not to your liking. But it will do until something better comes along. We need your wage coming in, with Davey gone and Gareth off sick.'

'No point in going, is there?' Olwen was twisting her hair behind her ears, trying to see her reflection in a tablespoon. ' 'What is your name?' she'll say, and when I tell her Rees, she'll ask, 'Ho! Any relation to the sinner who ran off with Miss Verity?' and show me the door so fast my feet won't touch the ground.'

'It could be a bit awkward,' Mam admitted. 'But I'm sending you up there for a purpose.

'Nothing at all has been heard from the Morgans, although Davey has been gone for a fortnight. Dada says Mr Morgan came to the pit head the other day on business, just as the men were standing by the shaft, waiting for the cage to take them down.

80

Mr Morgan knows your father well enough and Dada was waiting for him to say something — but he never said a word. I half expected the Morgans to turn up here looking for their daughter, but they didn't do that, either. I want you to go to the House and see what you can find out.'

* * *

Olwen set off to Cwmbran House the next day, clutching the reference provided by Miss Evans and looking rather nervous, as well she might.

By tea time she was back, with a tale to tell.

'I saw the housekeeper and she said that it was a lucky thing it was that I came today, for they are short a housemaid and I can start tomorrow. I came home to pack my things and I'll be off as soon as we've eaten.'

'But you gave your name as Rees?' Mam asked.

'Of course I did, but it didn't mean

anything to her.'

'Was anything said about Davey?'

'No, Mam.' Olwen sighed. 'Before I left, they invited me to have a cup of tea in the servants' hall, so I could meet the other staff. And there's clever I was. I asked how many of the family were in residence, and they said three. 'Mr and Mrs Morgan, and their little son, Peter. 'Is that all there is?' I said, and Cook told me there was a son in the Army, serving in South Africa, and Miss Verity, the only daughter.

' 'And where is Miss Verity now?' I asked. Cook said that she was home for a time but now she's gone again, taking Violet with her. And who might Violet be, I wondered, and they said she was the maid whose place I was taking. I saw some of them looking at each other and I thought it best not to say any more for fear of making them suspicious. I may hear something later if I keep my ears open.'

'So they don't suspect our Davey.' Mam sighed. 'Not for the moment, anyhow. You've done well, *cariad*.'

Olwen flashed her a rare smile, but Gareth looked thoughtful.

'I wonder what became of this Violet who supposedly left with Miss Verity? There was nobody with her and Davey at the station.'

'Perhaps she was in the guard's van, seeing to the luggage,' I suggested, but Gareth was not convinced. He remained thoughtful.

Olwen went off to Cwmbran House later that evening, in a happier frame of mind, fancying herself on a secret mission. Olwen Rees, heroine, was streets ahead of Rees, the parlour-maid. For once, Olwen seemed contented with her lot.

All this had to be kept from Mari, who could not be trusted to keep it to herself when she had schoolfriends to impress. Many of the pupils already knew that the Meistr had given me a Mizpah brooch. So she only knew that Davey had gone to work in Canada.

Now all we could do was wait. I knew

that Mam was hoping for a letter from Davey, but every day Jenkins the post went past our house without stopping.

Dada explained that it would be a long time before the runaways reached Canada, but Mam thought that he would surely write from Liverpool.

Olwen promised that if she found out anything before her first afternoon off, she would somehow let us know. We had to be content with that.

★   ★   ★

They say that troubles never come singly, and we were soon to learn the truth of that. I was surprised one day when a monitor came to my classroom to say that the Meistr had called an assembly of the whole school.

I could not imagine what Bryn's summons was all about, but I ordered my children into line and marched them into the next room.

When they had come to some semblance of order, Bryn came in and stood looking at the children in silence. I could tell by the way he looked that he was uncomfortable.

'You know that we are saving up to go on a trip at the end of the school year?' he began.

There were nods from many of the pupils. Each week their parents sent in what coins they could afford, and it was the responsibility of the teachers to make a note of the contributions before handing over the money to Bryn.

'I have been keeping that money in a cash box in my office and now I find that some of it has disappeared. I have counted it very carefully indeed, and there is no mistake. I have come to the conclusion that somebody has taken that money for themselves.' His voice was very serious.

The children were looking quite concerned now, and a few were red-faced. I knew from experience that this was not necessarily a sign of guilt, but an embarrassed reaction.

'You all know that stealing is a very wicked thing.'

There were more nods, and some of the bigger girls wore virtuous expressions.

'I don't know who has done this,' Bryn continued solemnly, 'but if they were a little older, they could go to prison. I'll say nothing more now, but I ask anyone who has anything to tell me about this matter to see me after school — or at least to return the money to my office.'

Later, Dilys and I discussed the incident with Bryn and Miss Edwards, who taught the older pupils.

'It must be one of the big boys,' Dilys remarked. 'Or girls. Who else would have the opportunity to go to your office, Mr Edwards?'

Miss Williams glared at her; the older boys were her charges, after all.

'It could not have happened in class time, surely?' I put in, as Miss Williams looked ready to explode. 'If a child went into the office, they'd know all about it.

They know it's out of bounds to them.'

Bryn nodded unhappily. He was fond of all the children and hated to think that any one of them could have behaved so badly.

I soon put the incident out of my mind, believing that it had nothing to do with me — but I could not have been more wrong.

The next day, just as I was preparing to leave for home, I was summoned to the office. There I had the shock of my life when I found a tearful Mari standing beside a triumphant Miss Williams. Bryn could hardly meet my eyes, but simply gestured towards Miss Williams, who was happy enough to step into the breach.

'When nobody came forward to confess, I had to do something,' she announced. 'After all, my whole class was under suspicion, and I could not have that. I set them a composition to write, and while they were thus occupied I went into the cloakroom and searched all the coat pockets. And what did I find in your sister's pocket? This, wrapped in a handkerchief!' She held out her hand, revealing a shilling and several smaller coins.

'No! There must be some mistake!' I exclaimed. 'Speak up, Mari! Tell me you don't know anything about this!'

But to my horror Mari stood with lowered head, reminding me of a daffodil drooping on its stalk.

'You see? The girl cannot deny it,' Miss Williams continued. 'Never did I think that a Rees could stoop to such a thing, and her own sister one of the teachers in this school. Shame on you, child.'

'Mari?' I pleaded. But still she said nothing.

'Get off home now, Mari,' Bryn said, not unkindly, and she ran from the room, sobbing as though her heart would break.

Bryn met my gaze at last. 'There's sorry I am, Gwen.'

Miss Williams snorted. She didn't dare to put her thoughts into words, but I could guess what was going through her mind — is Mari Rees to be let off because the Meistr is courting her sister?

'I don't know how I'm going to tell them at home,' I said at last. 'Poor Dada — Mari is the apple of his eye.'

In the end, Bryn wrote a note for me to take to Dada, saying he'd like to call on him that evening.

Mam was delighted when I handed him the envelope, and I was horrified to realise that she had jumped to the wrong conclusion — she thought that Bryn wanted to ask Dada's permission to marry me.

'No, Mam, it's not that,' I said quickly. 'It's about school.'

She was puzzled. 'But why tell Dada, then?'

'He'll explain when he comes,' I told her, my voice shaking.

She looked at my miserable face and patted my hand gently.

'There, there, *cariad*, it will all come right in the end.' Perhaps she thought I was about to be dismissed from my job!

At last Bryn arrived and the whole story came out.

'Of course she didn't do it! Did you, *fach*?' Mam cried, but there was no reply.

'Answer your mam, girl!' Dada thundered.

But it was useless. None of us could break her wall of silence.

Mari was sent to bed and Bryn went home. Dada saw him to the door, promising to get to the bottom of things.

'I believe the Meistr when he says the money was found in her pocket.' Mam said slowly. 'But anyone could have put it there.'

'Then why doesn't she speak up and tell us that?' I asked.

Neither of us could think of an answer to that.

Dada came back into the room and took his coat from the peg.

'I'm going for a walk,' he said. 'Too upset, I am, to settle.'

Verity's Letter

'Let me get in the door, then,' Olwen grumbled, kicking off her shoes. She'd been working at Cwmbran House for a week now and Mam was anxious for any news of Davey. 'I could do with a cup of tea! It's a long walk I've had, after working all week up there.'

Mam snatched up the singing kettle and scalded the pot, while Mari and I watched in silence. We were all agog to hear what Olwen had to say, but Mari was doomed to disappointment.

'Outside and play, *cariad*,' Mam ordered, and my little sister left the room without a word. Since her disgrace at the school, she'd crept about like a little mouse afraid of the cat.

'Well?' Mam demanded, handing Olwen a steaming cup.

'If you think I'm going to stay at that

old place for the rest of my days, you've got another think coming!' Olwen snapped. 'Work, work, work all day, with that housekeeper always after me, explaining things that any fool would understand!'

'Never mind that.' Mam was impatient. 'What about our Davey?'

Olwen shrugged. 'Never heard his name mentioned at all.'

'There must have been something said about Miss Verity, surely?' I put in. 'Where do the Morgans think she has gone to?'

'Well, at first they thought she'd gone off with Violet Pugh,' Olwen began.

'Violet Pugh?' Mam was puzzled. 'Who's she?'

'I told you before, Mam.' Olwen sighed. 'Violet was the maid whose place I'm taking. She and Miss Verity left at the same time and the Morgans assumed they went together. People like her always take maids with them when they travel, don't they?'

'But Gareth said there was no maid

when he saw them off at the station. Miss Verity left with our Davey.'

'I know, Mam, but the Morgans don't know that. Anyway,' Olwen continued, 'as it turns out, Miss Verity hasn't gone to Canada after all. The Morgans had a letter from her. She's staying with her Greataunt Euphemia in Scotland.'

'How would you know that? Surely you haven't been reading other people's letters?' Mam was shocked.

'No, Mam.' Olwen tutted. 'Mr Morgan had the letter at breakfast time. I was standing by the sideboard, playing the good little maid with my hands folded. I think he forgot I was there. He read bits of the letter out to Madam and, of course, I couldn't help hearing.'

'So what did Verity have to say?' Mam asked. 'Did you hear?'

'Oh, just that if she didn't want to get married, why should she have to? And forcing her into marriage with an older man, someone she didn't even know, was like something out of the Middle Ages.'

'And Violet?' I asked. 'She went with Verity, did she?'

'No,' Olwen said, biting into a tea-cake. 'The housekeeper noticed there were some valuable bits and pieces missing from a cabinet in the morning-room. Little silver things; snuff boxes and such.

'Our rooms were searched — servants are always the first to come under suspicion — but nothing was found. They came to the conclusion that Violet had taken the things and run off during all the fuss over Miss Verity's disappearance. It hasn't occurred to them that their precious daughter might have stolen the silver, of course!'

'Never mind that, Olwen,' Mam scolded. 'What about Davey? Gareth saw him with Verity Morgan.'

'Isn't it obvious?' Olwen sniffed. 'He and Miss Verity must have travelled together as far as Liverpool, then she went on to Scotland, while he boarded the ship to Canada.'

I couldn't bear the sight of Mam

dabbing her eyes with the corner of her apron. So often it seems that parents welcome their children into this world with joy, only to suffer grief by them in later years.

All I could think of was our Davey, going to the other side of the world. I still wasn't sure if he loved the wretched girl, or was just sorry for a pretty young woman in distress. Either way, I felt angry with Verity Morgan for having used my brother.

'Well, I can't sit here all day,' Mam said, tucking in a few strands of her hair which had come adrift from her bun. 'The men will be home soon, and me with nothing ready to eat. We'll have a letter from our Davey soon, I know, and then we'll hear the other side of the story.'

I followed Olwen upstairs to our room, where she flung her shoes into a corner and lay down with a sigh.

'Fetch me a bowl of hot water and some Epsom salts, will you, Gwen?' she pleaded.

When I had done so, Olwen sat soaking her feet in relief.

'I can't stand it up there much longer, Gwen,' she said, uncharacteristically quietly. 'I'm just not cut out for the life, scurrying here and there from six o'clock in the morning until last thing at night.'

'Try to stick it out a while longer, for Mam's sake,' I told her. 'Just until we know for sure that Davey is where they can't get at him. If they ever found out the part he played in all this, who knows what they would do, with Mr Morgan being a magistrate and all.'

She nodded, and promised to try. We might have had our differences in the past but when one of the family was threatened, we knew we had to pull together . . .

★   ★   ★

'Coming for a walk after chapel on Sunday?' Bryn had come into the classroom just when I was shrugging

96

my coat on, glad that Friday had come at last.

'I don't know.' I sighed. 'I don't feel like doing much these days, what with Davey running off and our Mari in such trouble.'

'Do you good, then, to get away for a bit. I thought we'd go up to the old abbey to get a bit of fresh air.'

'Fresh air!' I laughed. 'Get our heads blown off, you mean. What about coming over to the house for tea instead?'

'It's up to the abbey we'll go,' Bryn told me firmly. 'You need to blow the cobwebs away, Gwen Rees.'

So, Sunday afternoon saw us picking our way through the puddles to go up the mountain and at last we found ourselves at the dramatic ruins, gasping for breath. The wind had taken the pins from my hair and I must have looked like an illustration in Mari's book of folk tales with my hair blowing across my face.

As a child, I had been intrigued by the romantic atmosphere of this place. I had conjured up all sorts of tales around the piles of stones; knights rescuing fair damsels, strange creatures and magic spells. I remember Dada always listened patiently to my childish stories.

'Feeling better?' Bryn wanted to know, and I nodded.

I could not have guessed what he would do next! To my astonishment, Bryn got down on one knee and began to sing!

The tune was an old one, 'Venture, Gwen', in which a young man declares his love to his sweetheart, but Bryn's words were rather different from the original!

'Oh, come and be my bride,
Fairest Gwen, dearest Gwen!
For ever at my side,
Dearest Gwen!
Oh, say you'll leave me never,
We'll go through life together,
No matter what the weather,
Let us venture, venture, Gwen!'

I was laughing and crying at the same time, and I could only nod when Bryn asked what my answer would be. Welshmen sing in good times and in bad, so it was hardly surprising that the marriage proposal for which I'd waited so long should be set to music.

Bryn then reached into his overcoat, lying discarded at his side, and brought out a beautifully carved love spoon — the traditional gift from a lover to his sweetheart.

'I didn't carve it myself,' he explained quickly as I enthused over it. 'I'm not gifted in that way. I had Rhodri Mawr make it for me.'

I nodded. Rhodri lived beyond the mountain and was famous throughout the valley for his fine work. The spoon was decorated with delicate lattice-work, two intertwined hearts and a beautiful daffodil down near the bowl.

'Most people have the symbol of their work there, such as a lamb or a wheel,' Bryn explained. 'But I didn't know what to put for teachers. A cane, perhaps?'

We laughed happily, and as we made our way down the path, we were full of plans for the future.

I was rather taken aback when he spoke of the wedding taking place in a year or two. Why, I asked, had it to be delayed?

'As the Meistr, you live in the school house. It's not as if we have to move in with my parents, or save up to get started.'

But my cautious Bryn was firm. 'All very well to think of that now, *cariad*, but act in haste, repent at leisure.'

'You mean you're not sure you really want to marry me?' I said indignantly.

'Na, na. I only mean we should have something put by. What if something happened to me and I had to give up teaching? We would not have the school house then, and it would come hard on us if we had children. Better to be prepared.'

I could see that he was quite firm on the point, so I said no more. I had Bryn's declaration of love and that was more than enough . . .

Love was definitely in the air. I was sure that Gareth was working up his courage to propose to Dilys, my friend and fellow teacher. But I was careful to say nothing to her in case I had misread the situation.

Meanwhile, Dilys was thrilled for me.

'At last!' she said, knowing how impatient I'd been. 'And did he propose in a bower of roses, with violins playing?'

This was a reference to our girlhood dreams, when I had expected my lover to ride in on a white horse, like one of the knights of King Arthur.

Dilys had even more romantic ideas; she'd expected to be floating in a barge like the Lady of Shalott!

'We went up to the abbey and he asked me there,' I told her.

Her face fell. 'Not very romantic with a lot of old stones, was it?'

I smiled. No amount of teasing could spoil the glorious memory of Bryn's proposal.

'You won't mind where the proposal's made when the right man comes along, and I have a feeling that it won't be long now before he does!'

'Has he said something, then?' Dilys's face lit up.

I realised I'd gone too far — Gareth could do his own courting

'Who?' I asked innocently.

'Llew Roberts, of course!' Dilys said brightly. 'Come on, Gwen, you live right next door to the man, you must know something. There was a time when I thought he fancied you. Of course, that's all off now you're officially engaged, isn't it?'

I managed to change the subject. I'd had no idea that Dilys was still sweet on Llew — and what about our Gareth?

A few days afterwards, Gareth told me that he had asked Dilys to marry him. She had turned him down.

'There's sad, it is,' Mam remarked. 'I like Dilys, and would have made her welcome as a daughter-in-law. Gareth will be a good husband for someone, I know. Steady and hardworking he is.'

'I would have liked Dilys for a sister-in-law, too, Mam, but it seems it isn't to be.'

'Ay, maybe it's all for the best. A marriage without love is like a bird without feathers.'

I had to laugh at that, but the ache in my heart for my brother refused to go away. Never boisterous at the best of times, he now retreated into his shell, having no life outside the pit and the chapel.

* * *

One morning I was out shaking the mats when Megan called to me from next door. Leaning on the wall which separated our two backyards, she appeared more vivacious than usual.

'You'll never guess, Gwen,' she called. 'That friend of yours, Dilys, came round to see me last night, asking about our Llew. Quite smitten, she is — wants me to put in a good word for her.'

'And is he interested in her?' I asked warily.

'Well, I haven't said anything to him yet,' she admitted. 'At one time I hoped you and Llew might make a go of it, but he's had to give up that idea, hasn't he?'

'Dilys seems to have a good head on her shoulders. If she marries Llew and comes here to live, she can take care of Mamgu.'

Megan smiled. I knew Megan loved her grandmother dearly and was grateful that she'd taken in herself, her brother and her sister when their parents had died, but now that Mamgu was the one needing cared for in her old age, Megan was torn two ways.

'Then I'll be able to marry my Gwil and have a home of my own,' Megan continued.

'Why don't you marry Gwil and bring him here to live, then?'

'Mamgu doesn't like him,' she said simply. 'And anyhow, Llew has to stay here because this is a tied cottage. We're only able to rent it because he's a miner.'

During the weeks that followed, Dilys said nothing about Llew, and I assumed that Megan had failed to arouse his interest in my friend. I hoped he wasn't pining over me — it was bad enough seeing Gareth with a long face.

Already a lay preacher at the chapel, Gareth threw himself into the work of preaching at camp meetings through the area and this pleased Dilys's father, Reverend Parry.

For a time I didn't see Dilys outside of school because our occasional get-togethers at the Dragon tearoom had come to an end. I had cut back on treats because I was saving every penny towards my future home, and Dilys understood that.

There came a day, however, when she asked me to walk down to the shops with her after school. As Mam was short of potatoes and had asked me to collect some on my way home, I agreed to go.

'Is something the matter?' I asked, after Dilys had snapped at the girl in the greengrocer's for giving her the wrong change. It wasn't like her to be short-tempered or rude.

'Oh, it's Father as usual!'

'What has he done this time?' I knew how difficult Reverend Parry could be.

'He's trying to force me to marry Gareth.'

'What?'

'You heard. He wanted to know why Gareth has stopped coming to the house and, like a fool, I told him about the proposal.' She sighed. 'Father is very pleased with Gareth just now because he's going about preaching. Just the right sort of young man for me, he says.

'I tell you, Gwen, they're two of a kind, and I won't have it. Anyone I marry will have to come and live with us, because Father can't be left, and what kind of life would I have with two of them in the house?'

I was appalled. My brother was

nothing like Reverend Parry! I was cool towards Dilys after that and she realised it. Still, she made no attempt to apologise for her hasty words and I decided that I was not going to make the first move.

And so, after years of friendship, we parted on bad terms . . .

* * *

Because of her disgrace, the family decided that it was best to keep Mari home from school for a time, and Bryn agreed with Dada's ruling.

'She is not being expelled,' Bryn reasoned, 'as there is no real proof against her. But you must understand, Gwen, that until we get to the bottom of this, there is not much I can do.'

'I know,' I said unhappily. 'If only she would speak up. Mam insists that she is innocent, but Dada wants to know why Mari won't come to her own defence.'

I did not want Mari to fall behind in her studies, so her teacher, Miss

Williams, agreed to send work home for her to do. That term, the older girls were learning to knit, and Miss Williams wanted them to start on something simple, like a scarf for a member of their family.

Mam was happy to help with the project, but when Mari decided to knit a striped scarf for Davey, in the blue and white colours of the rugby team, they came to a parting of the ways.

Ferreting out an old blue pullover of Gareth's and a white knitted spencer of her own, Mam insisted that Mari should unpick the garments and use the wool. Mari was mutinous at the thought of all the extra work of unravelling and washing.

'All the other girls are having new wool,' she insisted. 'Why can't I go to Evans the draper and buy some? I'll be the only one in the class with this nasty old stuff.'

'You'll do as I say, my girl!' Mam snapped. 'You've plenty to say for yourself now, I notice, but not a word when Dada asks you a straight question about that stolen money!'

Mari went white, and went to sit in the corner where she began to pick at the blue pullover.

'I could have bitten my tongue out,' Mam admitted to me later. 'I want to believe that Mari would never dream of stealing, but what are we to think?'

We were all under a great strain and so it was almost with relief that I heard from Bryn that the thefts at the school had started again.

'One of the top form boys lost a florin from his desk,' he told me. 'His mother wanted him to run a message on the way home and he was foolish enough to leave the money in the classroom when I took the boys out for drill.

'Miss Williams was inside all the time, of course, taking the girls for knitting, but the thief must have taken the money when she was checking some child's work.'

'And Mari is at home so she can't be

responsible!' I put in gladly.

Miss Williams was brought into the discussion and it was agreed that no further action would be taken for the moment, in the hope that the thief could be caught in the act before long.

Bryn produced a shilling which he placed on Miss Williams' desk. The coin had a nick in it that made it easily recognisable.

In due course, the coin disappeared and when Bryn, hating every minute of it, searched the coats in the cloakroom, the missing shilling was found in the pocket of a garment belonging to Menna Pugh, a surly girl in Mari's class.

'That reminds me,' I told Bryn. 'You know that Olwen is working up at Cwmbran House just now? When she came home recently, she had some story about a maid who had stolen some valuables there — Violet Pugh. Any relation, do you think?'

'I wouldn't be surprised.' Bryn's voice was grim.

After school, Bryn accompanied Menna Pugh to her home on the Cwmbran Estate, where her father was Watkin Morgan's gamekeeper.

That evening, Bryn arrived at our house, looking relieved.

'When Pugh heard what his daughter had been up to, he was very angry. The girl has confessed everything, including the fact that she planted the coins in Mari's pocket so she would get the blame.'

Mam began to sniff happily, but Dada directed a stern look in Mari's direction.

'There must be more to this than meets the eye, Mari Rees,' he said. 'Out with it.'

Mari looked pleadingly at me, and then at Bryn, before blurting out the words she had kept back for so long.

'It was Menna, Dada,' she admitted. 'I saw her take the money from the Meistr's room and I said she had to put it back, but she wouldn't. She said if I told on her she'd tell everyone she saw

111

Davey in the wood all those times.'

'She saw Davey!' Dada cried.

'Yes, Dada, walking with Miss Verity. Menna's family have a cottage in the wood, and she meant to tell everyone that Davey and Miss Verity had run away together.'

'You have been a very silly girl, Mari,' Dada told her sternly. 'But everything has come right in the end. Now, isn't it time you went to bed? It's well past nine o'clock.'

Mari went upstairs looking as if the weight of the world had gone from her shoulders — and the next day, Mam went about the house singing once more.

Our troubles, however, were not yet over. Dada came home from work the next day, slamming his lunch pail down on the table and throwing his cap after it. Mam looked at him in surprise.

'Had a bad day, Huw?' she asked. 'Never mind, I have the water heating for your bath and a nice lamb stew waiting.'

'The meal will have to wait,' he told her. 'As soon as I get cleaned up, you and I have to go up to Cwmbran House, Susan.'

'Has something happened to our Olwen?'

'Nothing to do with Olwen,' Dada soothed. 'Waiting for the cage to take us down below, I was, when I was called to the office. The foreman has never liked me and seemed very pleased to tell me that we have been summoned by the Morgans, and must get up to the House as soon as work is over, quick, sharp!'

'It must be something to do with our Davey, then.' Mam looked worried. 'If they're dismissing you, the foreman would have turned you off then and there. And why do they want to see me? Are they giving us notice to quit the house, think you?'

But Dada had nothing more to say, and with instructions to me to feed Gareth when he came in, Mam untied her apron and went to brush her Sunday coat and hat.

I tried to get her to eat something while she was waiting for Dada to wash himself, but she shook her head.

'I couldn't eat anything, Gwen.' Her face was ashen. 'What can they want with us?'

At last, our parents were ready to leave. Mari and I stood in silence to watch them go.

'It's because of me, isn't it?' the child asked.

'Na, na, *cariad*,' I told her, putting an arm round her shoulders and holding her close. 'Dada will put it right, whatever it is.'

Mari was comforted and I was glad — but there was nobody to comfort me. Sick at heart, I closed the door.

Tempers Flare

When Mam and Dada returned home from the Morgans, it was evident from Mam's white face that things had gone badly while Dad's eyes flashed with annoyance.

'Make the dumplings, Gwen,' Mam instructed.

I did as she asked while they went upstairs to change into their ordinary clothes. I was desperate to know what had taken place, but I had to wait until they had eaten before they were ready to talk.

They had arrived at Cwmbran House where the housekeeper had showed Dada into Mr Morgan's study and informed Mam that Mrs Morgan would like to see her.

Dada and Mam had agreed beforehand to tell the truth as far as they knew it. 'Although perhaps not the whole truth,' Dada had said.

'Morgan started on me at once,' Dada told us. 'A friend of the family, who was seeing somebody off on the boat at Liverpool, had noticed Verity and Davey going aboard together. He was away from home for a time, but he told Morgan when he returned.'

'But they had a letter from Verity, Dada,' I interrupted. 'They knew that she was with her aunt in Scotland.'

'It was only thanks to Olwen's eavesdropping that we know of the letter, *fach*, so I could not mention it,' Dad explained. 'I told them that Davey had gone to Canada and it must be a coincidence that they were travelling in the same direction at the same time.'

'Oh, Dada!' Mari was wide-eyed. 'You told a lie.'

'Only a white one — and necessary.'

'But what did Mrs Morgan want with you?' I asked Mam.

'She has taken a liking to our Olwen and had wanted to take her with them to London,' Mam said. 'Her maid has arthritis in her hands, poor soul, and cannot do the work to Madam's satisfaction. Olwen was to be offered the chance to train in her place.'

I grinned, imagining what Olwen would say to that! Mam caught my eye and smiled before continuing her story.

'I said, 'That is very good of you, Madam. I was in service myself before I married and I should have liked to have been a ladies' maid.'

'She interrupted me and said, 'But, of course, that is not possible now, Mrs Rees, in view of what your son has done. I'm afraid that my husband insists that Olwen must leave our employ, although she must work out her notice just the same. I called you here because I wanted to explain that the girl herself is not in any kind of disgrace and I have no fault to find with her work.' '

I frowned. 'But what about the letter from Scotland?'

'There are ways and means.' Dada shrugged. 'Possibly the girl found someone who was travelling north and asked them to post it from over the border. The point is that she has gone to Canada with that fool of a Davey.'

'I wonder if they are married?' I said.

'What sort of wife would Verity Morgan make for a working man?' Dada sighed. 'Waited on by servants all her life, she probably doesn't know how to lift a broom.'

Mam brightened. 'The girl can learn, Huw.'

'Ay, she may have to. Morgan says he will cut her off without a shilling. And by the way he spoke, I wouldn't be surprised if the rest of us are dismissed along with Olwen.

'I tell you, Susan, I had great trouble holding my peace when the man spoke to me in that lordly way. Only the thought of the rest of you made me keep a still tongue in my head.'

Olwen came home the following week, smiling in delight at being released from the drudgery of working at Cwmbran House.

'The Morgans have gone to London. And you'll never believe this, Mam — the staff have been left behind with their wages reduced!'

'Board wages, they call it.' Mam nodded. 'It was the same when I was in service, *fach*. When the family is away there is less work for the servants.'

'Less work, is it?' Olwen sniggered. 'The Morgans may not be here to get waited on, but they want the house to get a thorough clean. All those heavy curtains have to be taken down and beaten, and the chandeliers taken apart and washed. And what about Cook? She still has to make meals for all of them.'

'Not seven-course meals like usual,' Mam said. 'Homely meals, like shepherd's pie and lamb stew, I suppose.'

Olwen smiled, pulling the pins out of her hat. 'Anyway, don't you worry about me, I have another job spoken for already.'

The new job was at the Black Lion Hotel, a temperance hotel, where people stayed overnight while breaking a journey.

'There's funny, it is,' Gareth teased, when he heard this news. 'My little sister, too good to skivvy for the Morgans, working as a chambermaid for strangers.'

'I'm to be in the dining-room for the moment,' Olwen told him, very much on her high horse. 'But when Miss Jenkins leaves to be married, I may learn to use the telephone switchboard, or even help at the front desk. The manager says a pretty face like mine will be an asset to the hotel.'

'Better not let Dada hear that kind of talk,' Gareth warned her.

Once again, Olwen left home, this time to take up residence on the top floor of the hotel, sharing a room with two other girls.

She did a stint as a dining-room waitress and, in time, did learn to answer the telephone. We all marvelled at that as there were very few telephones in Cwmbran at that time and those were mostly for the benefit of doctors and businessmen.

★ ★ ★

We were all looking forward to the Coronation of the new King the following summer. We knew that parties and picnics would take place then but, in the meantime, Bryn had suggested that a Coronation theme throughout the school year would make lessons interesting.

'What did you have in mind?' Miss Williams asked.

'Well, something about the British Empire, for instance, so the children can learn about the places ruled over by our new King, and the items produced there. As you know, Prince George and Princess Mary are touring the Dominions at this very moment, so there is sure to be plenty of coverage in the newspapers.'

'Could we look at some European countries, too?' Dilys asked. 'Queen

Alexandra comes from Denmark, and Princess Maud is married to the King of Norway.'

'What about making scrapbooks?' Miss Williams chimed in. 'My scholars are old enough to take an interest in current events and, as you say, Meistr, they can collect newspaper articles.'

I wondered what I could do for my pupils who were too young for these projects. I had already framed a picture showing King Edward and Queen Alexandra to hang on the wall.

That gave me an idea — we could make a scrapbook, too, with pictures of the royal children.

As the meeting ended, Miss Williams asked to speak to me.

'I am quite concerned about the friendship that has developed between Menna Pugh and your sister, Mari,' she told me.

'What friendship?' I stuttered.

This was news to me. It was not long since Mari had been accused of the thefts made by Menna Pugh; a friendship between the two of them seemed unlikely.

'Hand in glove, they are, Miss Rees, always together at playtime, and they have their heads together at dinner-time, sharing their food.'

What would Mam and Dada say? Apart from the grief caused to the family when Mari was in disgrace, the Pugh girls' aunt Violet had stolen articles from her employers, the Morgans of Cwmbran House.

Much as I hated to carry tales, I knew I had to say something at home. Surprisingly, Mam took the news in her stride.

'Good children are often attracted to the naughty ones,' she told me. 'They like to see others getting up to the sort of mischief they wouldn't attempt themselves. Do you remember that awful child you brought home to tea once? Angharad, her name was. I had a *teisen lap* cooling on the windowsill, and she made holes all over it with her fingers. Oh, my poor cake, and all that good fruit wasted.'

'Dada and the boys ate it anyway.' I grinned, remembering. 'And Angharad is a respectable wife and mother now, so she has grown out of her silly ways.'

'And so will Mari grow out of her affection for this Pugh child, if we make little of it. It will be just a passing phase.'

★   ★   ★

As time went on, I was troubled to learn that Olwen seemed to have become less careful of her reputation.

One Saturday morning I went to the Black Lion to deliver a jacket which Mam had been busy turning. The coat had once been mine and was due to be handed down to Olwen.

The cloth had faded badly and, consequently, looked shabby. Looking at the inside, Mam had declared it would be as good as new if she unpicked it and made it up again in reverse. True enough, the finished product was quite smart.

When I entered the foyer I was taken aback to find Olwen chatting and laughing with a gentleman — a commercial traveller by the look of him — and obviously neglecting her work.

Her face burned red when she saw me, and her admirer drifted away at the sight of my frown.

'Should you be quite so informal with the customers?' I asked. 'They might get the wrong idea about you.'

'I can look after myself, Gwen Rees.' Olwen's eyes flashed. 'And anyway, it's none of your business!'

'Perhaps I should make it my business. What would Dada say if he could see you now?'

'Oh, Dada! All he thinks about is work and chapel — and you're the same. What harm is there in having a friendly chat with the guests? This is a hotel, you know.'

Having said my piece, I thought it best to change the subject, so I opened the parcel and shook out the jacket. Mam had made a good job of it, and I half-regretted giving up the garment, except that it wouldn't go with my current wardrobe.

'More of your old cast-offs, I see!' Olwen curled her lip. 'Well, you can just take it back again. I'm making good money now and can buy nice things for myself.'

And indeed she did look very smart, in a long black skirt and white blouse. She was no longer required to wear the demure black frocks, aprons and white caps that the waitresses and chamber-maids wore.

I took the rejected jacket home again, saddened to see Mam's face after all her hard work.

'It will be useful for Mari in due course, I suppose.' Mam sighed.

Poor Mari, I thought. By the time she grew into it, the fashions would have changed — not that fashion played a huge part in the lives of the girls of Cwmbran!

*   *   *

My brother, Gareth, continued to preach at camp meetings on Sundays. Travelling by train or on foot, he would go to remote valleys, preaching in marquees or in the open air.

People seemed drawn to his gentle ways and earnest manner, and I suppose it was inevitable that he should win a small following of his own. He began to notice the same faces in the crowd wherever he went, and was encouraged when people came forward to shake him by the hand after the meetings.

Even so, we were not prepared for what happened next.

Mam was dozing in her chair when there came a knock at the door. I went to answer it and was surprised to find two rather common-looking women on the doorstep.

'Gareth Rees live here, does he?' the older one demanded.

'Yes, did you want to speak to him?' I asked politely.

'Not come all this way for nothing, have we, Betsy?' she said sarcastically, and the younger woman giggled.

'And who are you, Miss — not his wife, are you?' the woman continued.

'I'm Gareth's sister,' I said stiffly.

'Well, are you going to let us in?'

Mam was behind me now and the woman craned her head to look past me.

'Don't keep these ladies standing on the doorstep, Gwenllian!' Mam said, but the pair pushed past me before I could stand aside.

I could tell by Mam's tone that 'ladies' was not a term which came readily to her lips for these two. But, as visitors to our home, and possibly friends of my brother, they were to be treated with courtesy.

Gareth's face was a study as the pair swept into our kitchen. He and Bryn stood up as they entered, and I was annoyed to see that the women sank into the vacated chairs without being asked.

Gareth introduced them, looking most uncomfortable.

They were sisters from a village in the hills. The younger one was called Miss Betsy James and her sister was Mrs Blodwen Jones.

'And does your husband know you've come all this way?' Dada asked, when it became obvious that the two were reluctant to state their business.

'I buried him last year,' came the answer. 'Only a poor widow woman, I am. Life is hard for people like me, Mr Rees. That is why I take such comfort in the meetings, and the words of Gareth here.'

Conscious of her duty, Mam made a pot of tea and served homemade cake and biscuits, which the visitors praised lavishly. It was an awkward tea party, however. None of the family could find much to say.

When the last crumb had disappeared, Mrs Blodwen Jones looked at Gareth.

'Well, Mr Rees, our train won't go for

another two hours. Are you going to show us this famous town of Cwmbran, now that we have come all this way?'

Gareth mumbled something and I caught Mam making frantic signals to me. I gathered that the unspoken message was 'don't leave them alone!'

'We'll come with you,' I said brightly. 'Bryn and I were thinking about going for a walk when you arrived.'

'I think I'll stay here and help your mam with the washing up. She looks tired out, poor thing,' said Blodwen Jones.

'I can manage very well, thank you,' Mam said, but the irritating woman was already piling plates and removing crumbs.

With a shrug, Gareth led the way to the door and we were soon out in the fresh air, with Betsy James clinging to his arm.

'We could go up to the abbey,' I said, determined that if this intruder wanted a walk, she would have a long one!

But soon she was bleating and

limping, certain that blisters were coming up, so we decided on the park instead.

On our way through the town, we passed Dilys trudging up the hill. She stared at us in amazement. A scornful look came over her face when she saw the girl with Gareth, and I think she would have passed us by without a word if Bryn hadn't spoken first.

'*Prynhawn da*, Miss Parry.'

'Good afternoon, Mr Edwards,' she said, before scurrying off.

When I looked back over my shoulder, I saw that she was watching us. She tossed her head and looked away.

Dog in the manger, I thought. She has turned down Gareth's proposal of marriage, yet she's not best pleased to see him with somebody else in tow!

Gareth had a little smirk on his lips, and I guessed he was pleased by the little encounter.

Later, when we were back in Jenner Road and Gareth had gone to escort the two women to the railway station, I had a chance to complain to Bryn.

'Did you ever see such an awful pair? It was obvious Gareth had no idea they were coming — as if he would be interested in either of them!'

I walked Bryn to the door then, where we stood for a moment, entwined in each other's arms.

'Don't you worry about your Gareth,' he told me. 'He has a good head on his shoulders and is not likely to do anything foolish. You told me he's been a bit downhearted since Dilys turned him down, so it'll do him no harm to have two women in hot pursuit.'

'I suppose so,' I conceded. 'Did you see the look on Dilys's face when we met her in the street? Enough to sour the milk, it was.'

We laughed then, and parted with a kiss.

* * *

Coming home one day from a country walk with Bryn, I found Mam standing in the middle of the kitchen floor with a letter pressed to her apron bib and a look of joy on her dear, homely face.

'Davey?' I asked instinctively. 'You've had a letter?'

She nodded, hardly able to speak, and thrust the letter into my hand.

'*Dear Mam and Dada,*' I read. '*I hope this finds you well.*

I am living in a place called Toronto, which is not in the West but in the Province of Ontario.

On the boat coming over, there was a choir of Welshmen who are touring this country giving performances. They gave a concert on board and also sang at the Sunday service. It was grand to hear them singing their hearts out in the old language.'

'And he says a lot more,' Mam interrupted, 'all about the voyage and what they saw as they came into the Gulf of St Lawrence, all those little farmhouses and the churches with the silver steeples.

'But see what he says on page two.'

133

She snatched the letter from me and turned over the page, stabbing a finger at Davey's sprawling handwriting.

When we got off the boat at Montreal, I had planned to walk to the West to see about these farmlands, but I had not understood how vast this country is. Three thousand miles wide it is, and they told me it would take weeks to get to the other side, walking.

The Canadian Pacific Railway runs what they call colonist trains, taking newcomers to the West, but I had no money for that. It took almost all my savings to get this far.

One of the sailors on the boat is Welsh, and he says, 'Why not go to Toronto first? You can travel down with the choir and they will help you find the Welsh community there.'

So that is what I did. Think of this, Mam, there is a chapel here where they speak Welsh, and the people in the congregation help their own to get established when they first arrive in this country.

The minister has found me a job — just labouring for now but it will bring in some money — and I am living in a boarding-house with some other men and a landlady called Mrs Myfanwy Price.

I blinked at that. Nothing wrong with being a labourer, I thought; good honest work. Still, to go from being a skilled miner to digging ditches seemed a bit of a comedown. I said as much to Mam.

'Ah, but you have not seen what he says on the next page,' she told me proudly. 'He has it all worked out, *cariad* — my clever boy.'

Once again, she took the letter from me and handed me a new page, and I read it.

Reverend Bowen says that they have what is called a harvest excursion here in the autumn. Men can buy cheap tickets to go West to help the farmers there with the grain harvest. He says the experience will let me see if I like farming well enough to take up land as

I planned to do.

He thinks as Dada does, that it would be hard to homestead, as they call it, without capital, although the farmers are always glad to hire men to work for them.

'But see what he says about the mines,' Mam interjected. 'The minister says that Welsh miners are much in demand in the Western collieries, and Davey might be better to get work there.

The pay is better over there than here, or in Wales, and he says that some men go there just to get a little nest egg — a stake, they call it — and then they come back to Wales.

'Oh, Gwen, we may see the day when Davey comes back to us!'

I nodded. So much for Davey's longing to work above ground if he had merely exchanged one pit for another. Still, he was seeing the world, and the autumn farm work should be healthy enough.

I turned to the last page, which was marred by blots and many crossings out. Davey had obviously found it difficult to decide what he wanted to say.

You will know from Gareth that Verity Morgan has come to Canada with me.

I realise this must have been a shock for you all. I cannot tell you how many sleepless nights I've had, thinking of you. I should have had the courage to say goodbye face to face and to tell you of my feelings for Verity. But it is too late for all that.

Verity and I will try for a life together. We had thought of asking the ship's captain to marry us but, after talking to the sailor I mentioned before, we decided to wait.

Verity will remain in Toronto when I go to the West. I shall send for her when I have money in hand and a place to live. The journey would be too hard for her.

At present she is living in a boarding-house for ladies, run by a friend of Mrs Price. She will work in the house in return for her keep. She had a little money when she left Cwmbran, but she spent it on her passage. She could not be expected to travel third class, and share a cabin with another lady.

'At least he had sense enough to see that the girl cannot go with him to the West as things stand,' Mam said.

I had reservations, though. What sort of marriage would it be if Davey continued to treat the girl like a fine lady?

Verity had also plucked up the courage to write to her parents. That same day, my father was called to the mine office, where he found Mr Morgan pacing the floor.

'Red-faced, he was,' Dada told Mam. 'Ranted and raved, he did, shouting that I had failed to bring up my son in the right way.

' 'No morals, there,' he said, 'persuading a delicate young girl to elope with him to a foreign country.'

' 'And what about your daughter,' I said. 'Not kidnapped, was she? Went of her own free will, so what about her morals?' '

'Oh, Huw! There's foolish!' Mam was aghast.

'Ay, well, but somebody had to stand up to the man. 'You are walking on very thin ice, Rees,' he said, but I was past caring. He's sending someone to Canada to fetch his daughter back.

' 'I am glad to hear it,' I said, 'for the girl is not suited to be the wife of a working man.' Morgan glared at me then, and told me to get about my work. I went from the room without another word.'

Dada was not dismissed but Mr Morgan took his revenge in other ways. My father and Gareth were both transferred to the night shift 'until further notice'.

This was particularly hard on Dada, who did not sleep well in the daytime. It was hard on the rest of us, too, creeping about the house like little mice.

But there was more to come . . .

An Unexpected Visitor

We were just about to go to bed when there was a knock at the door.

Mam looked alarmed. It was almost ten o'clock and I knew what she was thinking — had there been an accident of some sort, involving a member of the family? It was the nightmare of every mining family.

I knew something was wrong as soon as I saw Bryn's face. It was unlike him to look so grim, and quite unexpected of him to arrive at that hour of the night. He went to the table and sat down heavily.

Mam, who had been banking down the fire for the night, made to leave the room, thinking that Bryn wanted to talk to me privately.

'Stay, Mrs Rees,' Bryn told her. 'You had better hear this, too.'

We took our places beside him.

'I had a message to go up to Cwmbran House this evening. I've come straight from there now,' he said. 'As you know, Mr Morgan is governor of the school, and his wife has always done a great deal for us. Now he wants me to give you notice, Gwen.'

'The coward!' Mam burst out. 'He can't even tell you to your face. The Meistr must do it!'

'But why, Bryn?' I could feel my heart thumping in my chest. 'What am I supposed to have done?'

'Do you have to ask?' Mam sounded bitter, which was out of character for her. 'He cannot reach our Davey, or his precious Verity, so the rest of us have to suffer now.'

'I'm sure he didn't put it like that,' I said.

'Oh, no!' Bryn's eyes were flashing now. 'No, he hinted that, being responsible for the school, he cannot employ someone whose morals may be in question.'

'What?' I was astonished.

'Of course I argued, Gwen — never think otherwise. His response was that all the Morgans are tarred with the same brush. He wanted me to let you go at once, but I insisted that you be allowed to stay until the end of the school year.

'It would cause talk if you suddenly disappeared in the middle of term, I told him. And it would ruin your reputation, both as a teacher and as a person.'

'Did he agree to that?'

Bryn looked at me sadly. 'He had to agree when I pointed out that he would be looking for a new headmaster as well,' he said quietly. 'I could not allow such an insult to the woman I am to marry.

'I gave him my own resignation, to take effect at the end of the year. He blustered, of course, but I will not condone such injustice.'

'Oh, Bryn! What are we going to do?'

Mam withdrew tactfully then, and Bryn and I talked far into the night.

Mr Morgan had agreed, for the good of the school, to say nothing about the resignations until the end of the year. We decided to do likewise.

'You would be leaving in any case when we are married,' Bryn reminded me, for married women were not permitted to teach. I was worried about Bryn being jobless, but he assured me that he would have no difficulty in obtaining a new post.

'Not in Cwmbran, though,' I reminded him sadly.

*   *   *

As I came up from the town, the lamplighter was making his rounds, reaching up with his long pole to turn on the gas in the street lamps. I had been to the library to change my books and, when I reached our street, I found that he had been there before me.

Mari had chalked a hopscotch game on the pavement and was playing amid the shadows cast by the light from the lamp two doors down.

'What are you doing out here?' I asked her, knowing that Mam did not like her to play out on the street after dark.

'There's a big argument in there,' she said, hopping breathlessly.

'Mam and Dad are arguing?' I was startled. It was a rare thing for our parents to quarrel. Mam was dedicated to keeping peace in the home, and Dada was slow to anger.

'Yes. It's Olwen.'

I sighed. So Olwen was home, and causing friction as usual.

'So you thought you'd better come outside, is that it?'

'Dada sent me out,' Mari muttered resentfully. 'There's silly, they are, treating me like a baby. I wanted to get on with my knitting and now there won't be time. As soon as they remember I'm out here, it will be up to bed.'

After many weeks of sighing and moaning, Mari had completed the striped scarf for Davey and in the process had come to enjoy knitting, which was now her favourite hobby.

'How are you coming along with the new project?' I asked.

She brightened. 'Almost finished now, it is.' Armed with fat wooden needles, and string saved by Mam from the parcels that had come into the house over the years, Mari was knitting a dishcloth, destined to go into my bottom drawer.

'And my teacher says it will be socks next term. I think Mam will let me buy new wool from Evans the draper, and I'll give them to Bryn for a wedding present.'

Just then, it started to rain.

'Come on, Mari,' I said. 'Dada would not want you out here in the wet. In we go, and straight up to bed with you. I'll bring you a nice cup of cocoa if you're quick.'

'And a biscuit?' she asked hopefully.

'Two!'

Dada looked up in irritation as we

came in, and Olwen shot me a furious glare.

'It's raining,' I told them, directing Mari towards the stairs.

As I mixed the cocoa to a paste and reached for the singing kettle, I could hear Olwen's voice raised angrily.

'Any other parents would be glad if their daughter got promotion after so short a time You were glad enough to push me off into service up at Cwmbran House. What's the difference now?'

'We did not push you off, as you call it,' Dada told her. 'You have to work for your living, we know that — but Swansea!'

'Swansea?' I repeated in surprise. 'That's a long way off.'

'It's a lovely new hotel, owned by Mr Richards, the man who owns the Black Lion,' Olwen explained, her eyes shining with excitement.

'He came to inspect our premises last week, and when he saw me he said how would I like to go to Swansea, to be one of the receptionists in the new place. The Red Dragon, it is called.

'Of course I should like to go — who wouldn't? See a bit of life and all the lovely shops and the sea. But Dada talks as if it is Sodom and Gomorrah all rolled into one!' She slumped in the chair, glowering.

As Dada glared back, a thought came to me.

'The Reverend Mr Parry comes from Swansea,' I began. 'Perhaps you could speak to him, Dada? He would know if the hotel is situated in a good district, and he might even know Mr Richards himself.'

'That would ease my mind, *fach*.' Dada nodded slowly. 'I'll speak to him after chapel on Sunday and see what he has to say.'

I was careful not to look at Olwen. Far from being grateful for my intervention, she would, I knew, resent the suggestion that Mr Parry be involved.

'Where is my cocoa?' Mari's plaintive cry wafted down from overhead, and I took the cup to my little sister, glad to escape from the argument.

⋆   ⋆   ⋆

Sunday came, and after the last hymn had been sung and the congregation dismissed, Dada made his way to the front and asked to speak to the Reverend Mr Parry in private.

'We'll go to the house, then,' Mr Parry said, and off we went with Dilys following behind in uneasy silence.

When we were established in the parlour, Mr Parry ordered Dilys to bring tea. Off she went to the kitchen, as meek as milk.

I have seen the time when I would have gone with her to help, but since her unkind words about Gareth, I could not bring myself to mend the breach.

Dada explained the situation and Mr Parry took charge at once.

'It is some years since I was in Swansea,' he began, 'and the town may be greatly changed.. Nor do I know this

Richards, although I have heard nothing spoken against him here. The Black Lion is respectable enough, I believe — a good temperance hotel.

'I have a cousin there, though — Reverend of the Bethel chapel. I shall write to him this very night and ask his opinion.'

The Reverend was true to his word and, within days, we had an answer.

'What does he say, Huw?' Mam asked.

'He has heard from his cousin, who says Richards has a good reputation and the hotel seems a decent enough place,' Dada explained after scanning the page. 'I suppose Olwen can give it a try. She can always come home if things are not as they seem.'

'But to go so far away . . . '

'It's not as far as Canada,' Dada reminded Mam, 'and Mr Parry's cousin has promised to take Olwen under his wing. Looking for good sopranos for the choir, they are.'

I grinned to myself. I didn't think

that singing in the chapel choir was exactly what Olwen had in mind.

Still, it would be good for her to widen her horizons and, as Dada said, she could always return home if things did not work out.

Another letter arrived from Davey in Canada and I read it aloud to the family, who were all eager to hear his news. He had travelled west, on one of the harvest excursions, and had plenty to say.

The train, filled with farm labourers, has taken several days to reach its destination, but the time did not seem long to me.

The countryside is so different from Wales. From time to time, the train stopped for several hours at a station, giving us the chance to stretch our legs.

Some of the men carried musical instruments with them and there was singing and even dancing in the aisles, for the carriages in the Canadian trains are not divided into compartments as they are at home.

*Each carriage has an iron stove in it,
heated by wood, and the boys take it in
turns to cook their meals on it.*

'There's funny, it is.' Mam laughed.
'To think of our Davey doing his own
cooking!'

Davey also described the endless
acres of land in the prairies, with never
a habitation in sight. It was hard for us
to grasp the vastness of what, to us, was
an alien land.

'The boy sounds happy enough,'
Dada commented, sucking on his pipe.
'Hard work never hurt anyone, and I
suppose that cutting peat out there is
no different from back here.'

'And the family he's staying with
sounds all right,' I put in.

Davey had written that they were
hard-working Ukrainians. The farmer,
Rauliuk, seemed good-hearted.

The women of the household produced enormous meals — simple, plain
food — and when they were not
cooking and baking they took their
place in the fields with their menfolk.

A neighbour who spoke English told Davey that when Anthony Rauliuk had first taken up the land, he was so eager to prepare it for seeding that he had hung a lantern from his horse's head so as to continue ploughing throughout the night.

'Those poor men,' Mam remarked. 'A hard life it is for them, indeed. That Verity Morgan is well out of it in Toronto.

'But, Gwen, I could hardly believe what he had to tell us about the houses there. Soddies, he calls them. Only huts they are, with the roof made of sod cut from the earth. Does that keep out the rain? Or is there a shower of mud over everything on a wet day? Indeed, I rue the day we let our Davey go!'

'As I recall we did not have the chance to hold him back,' Dada said mildly. 'And Davey has already told us that there are many fine houses built from brick or stone in Toronto, as well as those wooden ones — what was it he called them, Gwen?'

'Frame, Dada.'

'And he also said that when the pioneers first came to Canada they cut down trees and made their house out of logs, because they were free. No doubt it is the same with the sod houses. The people will build better homes when they can afford to do so.'

'Afford or not — ' Mam sniffed ' — even the beasts in Wales have better houses than our Davey just now.'

Bryn was very interested to hear of these strange houses.

'Just the other day I was teaching the older boys something similar,' he explained. 'Not so long ago in Wales, if people could erect a dwelling overnight and take up residence by morning, they could keep the land it sat upon.'

'And I have read that before these new Canadians can have title to their land, they must clear a certain acreage and put up a house,' Dada put in. 'It's not so very different from what you are saying, Bryn.'

'I still say it is not right,' Mam said,

'to live like a *buwch yn y beudy*.'

'Ah, but do they have a house for the beasts at all?' Bryn teased. 'Or do they share the little houses with the people? Keep you warm at night, it would, an nice big cow!'

Mam flapped a hand at him in exasperation, but she was laughing as she went to peel the potatoes for tea.

I noticed that Gareth was deep in thought.

'You should go out to Canada and join Davey.' I smiled. 'If you want to escape Betsy and Blodwen!'

The two women from the next town considered Gareth quite a catch — and made little secret of their intentions!

'I don't know what you mean.' But Gareth's face was crimson.

'It's not every man has two fine women in hot pursuit.' Dada laughed, joining in the fun. 'And you cannot wed them both.'

'I have no liking for either one,' Gareth said between gritted teeth, 'but they will not be shaken off. There's

155

tired I am of their following me and tired, too, of being teased by the likes of you.'

'Better go to Canada, then,' I said. 'They can't follow you there!'

⋆   ⋆   ⋆

The gamekeeper's daughter had been asked to exercise the pony belonging to the youngest Morgan — Master Peter — while the family were away. The animal was too small for any of the grooms to ride, being barely twelve hands high.

At Menna's insistence, Mari pestered Dada to let her go to Cwmbran House to learn to ride.

I could sympathise with her. When I was her age, I had been very envious of Miss Verity, whom I had seen trotting through the town on a fine Welsh pony, accompanied by a groom. Oh, how I'd longed to be like her!

I remember telling Mam about this, but she only smiled.

'If wishes were horses, beggars would ride,' she told me.

Dada finally gave in to Mari. 'I will go to see Pugh. If it is true that Menna is supposed to exercise Master Peter's pony, and if you will not be in the way, perhaps it will be all right.'

Pugh gave his approval, Dada gave permission, and Mari went off to Cwmbran House in great excitement.

She was back by tea-time, full of her adventures.

'Out to the scullery and have a good wash,' Mam insisted. 'You are not coming to my table smelling of horse!'

I followed her out with a kettle of hot water in my hand.

'How did you like riding?'

'I liked the horse, but I did not like that old groom.' She pouted. 'Shouted at me all the time, he did.'

'Whatever for?'

'He said we had to stay in the stable yard for the first time, to make sure we knew what to do.'

'Quite right.'

'I was sitting on the pony — Pickles, its name is — and Menna was leading it, and that's when the man started to shout. 'Head up, hands down, elbows in, heels down, grip with your knees!' '

'You seem to have learned something, anyway.' I was trying to hide a smile.

'That stuff may be all right for Master Peter when he goes in for gymkhanas,' Mari told me importantly. 'Menna and me, we only want to ride for fun.'

'You'll get fun when Mam sees that great potato in your stocking,' I said. 'Hurry you now and get washed. Gingerbread for tea!'

It was a terrible shock to us when, after one of these Saturday excursions, there came a pounding at the door and we found Mr Pugh on our doorstep, holding Mari.

One boot was missing, her pinafore was smeared with green slime and there was a deep gash on her forehead. Her hair was in rats' tails and she looked as if she had been dragged through a hedge backwards.

'Take your sister upstairs, Gwen,' Mam ordered, taking charge. 'And get her out of those soaking clothes. Come in by, Mr Pugh.'

I helped Mari to our room. She was shaking with cold and shock, and I had a difficult time peeling the sodden garments off her because she could hardly lift her arms.

When she was towelled off and wearing a thick flannel nightgown, I tried to put her to bed, but she insisted on going down to the kitchen.

'Sad it is, Mrs Rees,' Mr Pugh was saying, 'when you bring up your children to be upright citizens, yet they bring shame on your head.'

Apparently the girls had taken the pony into the woods, which they were now allowed to do, provided one led the animal while the other rode.

Ceinwen, Menna's younger sister, had wanted to go, too — but Menna had taunted her with being too young.

She had made up her mind to get her own back. She had hidden behind a tree and waited for them to pass — Mari on Pickles and Menna leading him. When they came level with her, she had jumped out, screaming.

Pickles had shied, jerked free of Menna's guiding hand and galloped off, with Mari clinging to the pommel of the saddle.

When Menna finally caught up, she found Mari lying half stunned in the river. She screamed at Ceinwen to fetch help and, terrified by what she had done, the child ran for her father.

'I wanted to take the child to my wife,' Pugh told Mam, twisting his cap in his hands, 'but she kept moaning and saying she wanted to come home to you. I carried her all the way, Mrs Rees. I hope I did the right thing.'

In the circumstances, I thought Mam was showing great restraint in merely thanking him for his help. I would not have blamed her if she had given him a piece of her mind for not having better control of his daughters.

'You wait until your father gets home,' Mam snapped when the door had close behind Mr Pugh. 'There's cross he will be when she sees the state you are in.'

Mari burst into fresh sobs. 'It was not my fault, Mam,' she said. 'It was Ceinwen. You can't blame me. It's not fair!'

★ ★ ★

At school next day, young Ceinwen watched me with wary eyes. As far as I was concerned, it was just a piece of childish mischief which had gone wrong, but I was not about to tell Ceinwen that. She was the class mischief-maker, and her actions were all too often malicious.

Perhaps this episode would teach her a lesson, I thought — though I had my doubts!

'There you are, Miss Rees!' Miss Williams said when I told her what had happened. 'Didn't I tell you that no good would come of this friendship between your sister and Menna Pugh? I hope that your father will see sense now and put a stop to this nonsense.

'Pony riding, indeed! That is all very well for the Morgans, but girls of this age would be better occupied learning to cook and sew.'

Mari developed a nasty cold, and Mam tried her home remedies and tasty dishes to tempt the child's appetite.

She had always had a weak chest, so it was no surprise when she developed a nasty cough, and all Mam's ministrations with goose grease and red flannel had no effect.

One evening, Mam spoke very worriedly to Dada.

'The child is very feverish, Huw,' she said quietly. 'I think you should go for the doctor.'

Dada went at once and was back with the doctor within half an hour. We listened with dismay to the doctor's words.

'Pneumonia, I'm afraid,' he told us. 'We shall have to be very careful of the child, Mrs Rees.'

He had no need to tell us that. We knew that people died of pneumonia, and Mari was none too strong to begin with. We listened numbly as he gave instructions to Mam, and explained that he would arrange to have a trained nurse move into the house.

'But I want to look after Mari myself!' Mam protested.

'Of course you do, Mrs Rees, and you shall play your part. But this is serious business, and someone with experience must be brought in to deal with it.'

After that, all our troubles appeared as nothing, as we waited to see whether Mari would live or die . . .

Good News And Bad

Within hours of the doctor's diagnosis, Nurse Beynon had moved in with us to look after Mari.

She removed her long navy blue, red-lined cloak to reveal a serviceable grey dress which, not quite reaching the floor, allowed a glimpse of shining black boots and black stockings. From that moment, kindly and efficiently, she took charge of the household.

After tucking a stray curl under her starched white cap, she put on a white apron which crackled with starch.

'Now,' she said, adjusting the bib, 'shall we begin?'

Angels come in many guises, and Mam was so pleased that someone was caring of Mari that she raised no objection to taking orders from the nurse. Meekly she did everything that Nurse Beynon asked — and I was her faithful lieutenant.

'Where is my patient? Upstairs?' the nurse asked. 'Well, that won't do for a start. Too much running up and down, see? What about your parlour, then? Can your husband put up a bed in there?'

'Two beds in there already, there are,' Mam told her. 'My son, Gareth, sleeps there, and so did his brother, Davey, before he went to Canada.'

I was sent next door, and Megan readily agreed to let Gareth move in and share Llew's room for the duration. By the time I returned, Mari was installed in Gareth's bed, Mam was busy laying a fire and the nurse bustled about as if in a hospital ward.

When I went to school the next day, I was given a list of items to shop for on my way home. Even though Nurse Beynon could be left in charge, Mam was determined not to leave the house for a moment.

I had to find arrowroot, Friar's balsam and bones to make broth, so I needed to visit a number of shops. I was grateful when Bryn told me to leave school early.

'I will keep an eye on your pupils,' he told me, his brow creased with anxiety on my behalf.

I trotted off, feeling somewhat guilty. I could imagine my fellow teacher, Miss Williams, nodding meaningfully at Dilys. 'Special treatment, you see, Miss Parry,' she would say. 'Engaged to be married to the Meistr!'

Mari's condition went from bad to worse. Nurse Beynon was forever sponging her down, forcing medicine into her protesting mouth and performing mysterious rituals which we could barely understand. She was at Mari's side day and night, only snatching a few hours' sleep or a quick meal when Mam would take her place.

Mari's bedclothes were constantly damp and Mam herself was kept busy with extra washing. Megan volunteered to launder Gareth and Dada's pit clothes.

'Doing it already, I am, for our Llew,' she said cheerfully. 'What are a few more bits and pieces? Your Mam cannot put coal-black clothes and the white wash in the same water, can she?'

I knew that Megan was taking on more than 'a few bits and pieces' and was grateful. The men's grime-encrusted clothes gave rise to hard work on the wash-board, as I knew from experience. We had a difficult enough time drying everything as it was, and soon ran short of bedding.

'There's awful, it is, making poor little Mari lie on this old sheet that is turned sides to middle,' Mam lamented. 'It has a seam right down the middle, right where she'll lie.'

'Better a patch than a hole,' I said, quoting the old proverb. 'Now, you are going to put your feet up on a stool while I make you a nice cup of tea.'

Mam was too exhausted to put up an argument.

'Better take one in to Nurse Beynon, too.'

This done, I sat beside Mam while she gazed into the fire, letting her tea grow cold.

'The child is no better,' she murmured, her voice very low. 'I'm beginning to think there is no hope for her, Gwen *fach*.'

'There is always hope, Mam.'

'Yes, there's always hope, but in the end it must be as the Lord wills. I know that, Gwen, and I like to think that I have a faith that would move mountains, and yet I do not think I could bear to lose another child.'

My heart went cold. 'Another child, Mam?' I asked, confused. 'What do you mean?'

She stared into the leaping flames for a few moments before speaking.

'I suppose I have never mentioned this, Gwen. It happened before you were born. Gareth had a twin brother, Hywel his name was.'

I gasped. This was something I'd never heard before.

'When my time came, Huw went for

the midwife, but she was already attending another woman and couldn't come. He was afraid for me, so he went next door and got Mair Roberts. She did her best, but she had no nursing experience.'

'You must have been so afraid . . . '

'Na, na. With the pains upon me I had no time for that. It was poor Mair who was afraid — she was expecting her own first child . . . '

'Poor Mair.'

'Well, Gareth was safely born and then we were surprised when another baby made his way into the world. That was Hywel.

'Only an hour he lived, poor little boy. You're lucky, they all told me, you have the other *baban*. But still I grieved over the little lost one.'

She was silent for a while before she went on. 'The next year, we had Davey. I thought to name him Hywel but Huw said no, this was not Gareth's brother come back to life but a new child. So we called him Dafydd, after Huw's brother that died young.'

I knew that it was common for many families to lose a child or two, not that it was any consolation to the grieving parents.

'I believe that our new King and Queen had a baby boy who lived for only a day,' I murmured. 'Little Prince Alexander John.'

'Yes,' Mam said thoughtfully. 'It happened just a few years before I lost Hywel. I think of that often, even after all these years. The royal family must have the best doctors in the world, and yet they still have their troubles like the rest of us . . . '

* * *

The day came when Mari did not know us. Tossing restlessly in her bed, she cried out for Mam, yet was not comforted when Mam smoothed her brow and spoke soothing words in her ear. I couldn't bear to meet Mam's eyes at these times.

170

Nurse Beynon kept copious notes and details on a graph which charted Mari's temperature, pulse and respiration.

Once, I stole a look at this chart, but couldn't understand it properly. The lines went up and down in mountains and valleys, reminding me of the map at school, showing the terrain of Wales.

Nurse Beynon came back and caught me looking at the chart, but she wasn't cross. She explained gently that her patient was going through a series of crises as the body tried to fight off the disease.

'I expect the real crisis to come tonight, Miss Rees, and then we shall see.'

Mam had come into the room just then, and asked what she meant.

'I mean that if she comes through the night, then there is hope for recovery,' the nurse replied.

And if she does not? I couldn't help thinking the question — but I did not dare to say it aloud.

171

★ ★ ★

Another letter came from Davey. It made for exciting reading, and Gareth said it reminded him of the stories in the 'Boy's Own' paper.

Bryn came over in the evening to sit with me — he understood that I did not want to leave the house while Mari was so ill — so he elected to spend time in Jenner Road as a show of support. He and Gareth sat with their heads together, speaking softly so as not to disturb the invalid in the next room.

'I would let you read the letter for yourself, Bryn,' Gareth told him, 'but Mam keeps it in her apron pocket and will not let it out of her sight. As long as she has it there, she believes she's keeping Davey safe from harm.'

'And what is he doing now there's no work on the farm?' Bryn wanted to know.

'He is serving in what they call a hardware store — that's an ironmonger's shop to us. He could have gone back to the farm to help with the spring seeding, but the winters are so long there, lasting five or six months, with several feet of snow over all the land.'

'But does he mean to stay at the shop?'

'Na, na. It is just to tide him over, he says. They need men to work there because of all the heavy lifting. The shop sells lumber, ploughs and wagons, as well as the usual things.'

'Tell him about all the settlers coming in,' I put in, waving at them with the stocking I was darning.

'People are arriving in droves,' Gareth told us. 'Riding in wagons piled high with stoves and furniture and bedding, with little children perched on top of the load. Some people come west by train in what they call the colonist cars, and they buy wagons when they arrive and load everything on at the station.

'Some are Americans driving covered wagons like we saw in the 'Boy's Own'. It must be quite a sight to see all those people crossing the countryside in a long line.'

'You forgot about the tent, Gareth.'

'The tent, yes.' Gareth laughed. 'One man had pitched a tent on top of an ordinary hay wagon. There's ingenious, he was, it would save his family getting wet, I suppose.'

I sat quietly in the firelight, thankful to be sheltered under a good slate roof. The pioneer life was not for me, I thought. Imagine travelling hundreds of miles in an old wagon, getting off in the middle of nowhere to live in a hut made of turf, and having to tame the unbroken land before the first crops could be planted.

'Does Davey still hope to get a farm of his own?' Bryn wondered.

'It's hard to say. He has been advised that any settler who comes in with less than three hundred dollars behind him should work for a year or two to get a stake, as they call it.

'A team of good horses and farm machinery costs money and the climate is such that many things can go wrong with the crops. Davey says that he will go back to working in the mines out there,' Gareth continued. 'The pay is better and it's what he's used to. He's going to visit one of the collieries this week and see what jobs are going.'

'He must have done that by now,' Bryn mused. 'His letter would have been a long time coming. First crossing the continent by train and then coming on by ship and then by train again from Liverpool.

'That might make an interesting lesson in geography for the older ones at school, Gwen. We can show them Davey's letter, or the envelope, anyway, and get them to trace its journey on the map.'

'Or write a composition,' I put in, ever the teacher.

Gareth stood up and took a turn around the room before coming to rest beside the fire, leaning on the mantelpiece.

'I have always been sorry that I didn't

go to Canada with him,' he said, drumming his fingers on the face of the clock. 'Not to go off like he did, of course, without waiting to say goodbye. Now, I think it would be good to go.

'I'll wait and see what our Davey has to say about the mines. If there is a job for me, perhaps I shall go after all.'

'Don't let Mam hear you say that,' I murmured, glancing fearfully over my shoulder at the closed door behind which the two women were fighting for Mari's life.

'Na, na, Gwen, I'm not such a fool. There's still time.'

'You'll go in for farming later on, then, and apply for some of that free land?' Bryn asked.

'All in good time, boyo, all in good time.' Gareth shrugged. 'For the moment, I want to see a bit of the world, work in a different pit for a change, and have new experiences. I can always come back in a year or so if I want to.'

'And you can escape from Betsy and

Blodwen at the same time,' Bryn said, with a twinkle in his eye.

'Maybe I should take them along, to cook!' Gareth laughed.

I smiled at their banter as I bent over my work. Mam was right in referring to the two women as bold hussies, I thought.

They were still relentless in their pursuit of my elder brother. Even over the long winter, when the tent meetings had been cancelled, they travelled down from their valley every other Sunday afternoon, to call on us — despite the fact that no invitation had ever been made!

One time when they had arrived at the door, simpering and preening, they were sent on their way by Dada, who informed them in no uncertain terms that there was illness in the house and that Gareth was away from home.

Even then they were reluctant to leave, saying with a pout that they needed the spiritual consolation which only Gareth could impart.

'Then I suggest you call on the Reverend Mr Parry. He will surely understand you, being a widower himself.'

With that Dada shut the door and the pair strode off down the street, heads held high.

'I hope they do call on Mr Parry.' I giggled. 'Short change he'll give them, I'm sure.'

'And it's all they deserve,' Dada said, with a twinkle in his eye.

It was late before Bryn left that night. He and Gareth had become close friends, and they could easily talk about anything and everything well into the small hours.

As Gareth made his way to bed, I decided to stay up and help Mam with Mari, but she insisted that I go to bed.

'Nurse Beynon and I will be keeping watch, *cariad*, and you have to get up for school in the morning. Get the cane from Miss Williams, you will, if you're late.' She gave me a faint smile and I was glad that she could make a small joke, even while she was so worried.

I went to bed, but I didn't sleep well. I had wild dreams in which Nurse Beynon was speeding across the Canadian prairies in a covered wagon . . .

I was awake at dawn and, after tossing and turning in an unsuccessful bid to get back to sleep, I decided to give in and get up. Taking my wash jug from the stand, I tiptoed downstairs, meaning to fetch some hot water. I soon forgot the water, however, when I found Mam standing in the kitchen, gripping the fire guard with both hands, weeping soundlessly.

'Mam?' I asked, concerned. 'Is it Mari?'

'She came through the night, Gwen.' Mam nodded. 'Nurse Beynon says she has turned the corner.'

'Oh, Mam!'

My hands began to shake uncontrollably and I had to put the jug down on the table with great care, lest it fell to the floor and broke.

Then we clung to each other in the

quiet of the dawn and cried happy tears.

★ ★ ★

Mari gradually grew better and at last, of course, Nurse Beynon had to leave. We were sorry to see her go, but Mam was pleased to be in sole charge of Mari once again.

'We must feed her up,' she declared. 'Her poor little face is so pale and thin, like two holes in a blanket.'

But Mari had no appetite and the doctor told Dada that she must go away to a convalescent home for a few weeks. Mam protested, of course, but the doctor was insistent.

'Sea air is what those poor lungs need now, Mrs Rees, not coal dust. We do not want to leave her with a weak chest for the rest of her life, do we now?'

'But to go so far away from us all, Doctor,' Mam pleaded. 'Whatever will the poor child do? And those places only allow visitors once a week so it would do no good for me to stay nearby.'

'What about that other girl of yours, Olwen? Isn't she working in Swansea now? There's a convalescent home not very far away. If I could get Mari in there, she would have her sister to visit her.'

So it was arranged that Mari was to go to Swansea when she was well enough to travel.

Olwen came home to collect her, looking very smart in a new costume and big cartwheel hat. Mari went with her, rather pale and apprehensive, but we had every faith that our little sister would be home by summer, fully returned to heath.

After all the emotional upset, I felt quite drained and looked forward to a quieter time. Once a week, Mam and I wrote letters to Mari in the convales-cent home, which we posted in separate envelopes so she would have the fun of receiving two letters instead of one.

Mam also wrote to Davey in Canada.

We had no exciting news to tell, but we reckoned that our young exiles would appreciate the link with home.

Mam was pleased when another letter came from Davey, but was disappointed with the contents.

'All about some old coal mine, Gwen,' she said. 'Here, you can see for yourself, but you will not be interested. We hear enough about the work as it is, with Dada and Gareth in the house!'

But the men were interested and discussed the contents eagerly. Davey had the promise of work in a place called the Crowsnest Pass, and was full of information about what he had seen at a mine there.

The men use the Davy Safety Lamp, he had written. The mine company keeps the lamps in good working order and they have men to clean the lamps after each shift. Each miner is issued the same lamp each day, which he must return to the lamp house, and this acts as a safety precaution because they can tell at once if anyone is missing.

Mam was rather envious of the fact that 'Davey's mine', as she called it, had a bath-house where the miners could wash themselves and change into clean clothes before heading for home.

'There's nice it would be not to be heating water for the old tub,' she remarked. Our men still had to cram themselves into the small galvanised bath in front of the fire, shielded from view by the clothes-horse draped with an old blanket.

The mine employs many men, Davey had continued, including all those who work underground, and others who work at the picking tables, sorting the coal from the slack. The owners want to hire more skilled hardrock miners as tunnellers and plan to hire Welshmen, like ourselves, for the purpose.

'And see, it is all day work,' Dada commented. 'The boy says that a tunneller will get more pay than the rest, and a man to assist him. Gareth — if you are going out there to work, now is your chance.'

'No more talk about going to Canada, Huw Rees!' Mam frowned.

'Oh, leave the boy alone, Susan. If I were twenty years younger, I would think of going myself. See a bit of the world, make some money. If Gareth wants to go, now is the time before he thinks of marrying and settling down.'

Gareth's eyes flashed, but for once Dada was not teasing him about Betsy and Blodwen and my brother calmed down.

'I think I shall go,' he told me later. 'Perhaps Dilys is right — I am an old stick in the mud.'

'No, no, Gareth, steady is all.'

'Too steady, is it? She made me think, Gwen. I am too cautious by half. I wonder now, when I was younger and wanted to be a doctor, did I give up too easily? Other working men manage it somehow, but I just gave up and went down the pit instead.'

He repeated those words when Bryn called in later, and I was surprised when Bryn agreed with him.

'It would be good to see a bit of the world while you are young,' he enthused.

'But wait until you have something more saved,' Mam said. 'What will you live on until you get your first wage packet?'

'I can stay with Davey, Mam. He says there are little towns growing up around the mines and there is room for me in the boarding-house where he is going to live.'

'He doesn't mention Verity,' I remarked. 'I thought they would have been married by now.'

'I suppose she is still working in Toronto, waiting for Davey to save enough to pay her train fare to the West,' Mam mused. 'And even after she joins him it will not be roses all the way.'

'There's glad I am that I am not going to marry a miner,' I told Bryn. 'No fear of you going out to Alberta.'

I was taken aback when his face reddened.

'Get your hat, *cariad*. I have something to tell you.'

* * *

In silence, we walked until we had reached our favourite spot on the hill, overlooking the town. There, he took me in his arms, and we enjoyed the view together for a few moments.

'Gwen,' he said softly at last. 'I am going to Canada with Gareth.'

'But you are not a miner, Bryn!' I protested.

'No, but I am a school-teacher, and you know that I have to find a new job,' he explained calmly. 'I have applied for a post in Saskatchewan, which is not as far to the west as Alberta, but still on the prairies. I read an advertisement in 'The Echo', for a man who can teach in Welsh.'

'And you did not find it necessary to discuss this with me, Bryn Edwards?' I could feel the anger rising in me.

'I could not say anything while Mari

186

was so ill,' he said patiently

'How could you do this to me?' I blurted out. 'We are supposed to be getting married, or had you forgotten that?'

'No, I have not forgotten that, Gwen. I thought we could marry before I go, so that you can come with me.'

This took the wind out of my sails, but I was still far from calm.

'Did you think I would be happy to hear this?' I hissed. 'Tell me you are not serious about this!'

Bryn was dumbfounded and stared at me in bewilderment.

'I am going home now, before I say something I shall regret!' I told him. 'I am not leaving Wales, and that is that!'

I marched off without looking back. I couldn't believe what Bryn had just said! It was true that he had to find another job, but surely there was no need to go all the way to Canada!

A New Life

My parents looked up in alarm when I marched into the house, breathing fire. Bryn was at my heels.

Thoroughly worked up, I did not give anyone the chance to speak.

'Bryn has made plans to go to Canada with Gareth. He expects me to drop everything to go with him!'

'Nothing is settled yet, Mr Rees,' Bryn interrupted quickly. 'I have applied to go to Canada to teach in a school where a Welsh-speaking master is required. If I am successful in obtaining the position, Gwen and I can be married and go out there together.'

Mam stole a worried glance in my direction, but said nothing.

'But why do they want a teacher who speaks Welsh?' Dada wanted to know. 'I thought English and French were the main languages over there. Is there to be a new school in Toronto, where Davey attended that Welsh chapel?'

'This is for a new settlement which is to be founded in the province of Saskatchewan, made up of people from Patagonia.'

'Patagonia?' Dada leaned forward, his face alight with interest.

I could see that I would have to remain quiet if I wished to learn more, so I slid into a seat beside Mam while Bryn stood with his back to the fire, as if about to give a lecture.

He had no need to tell us about Patagonia, for the tale was well known. Back in 1865, when Mam and Dada were children, there had been a resurgence of Welsh nationalism, and a large group of people had gone away to start a new life in Argentina.

Despite some initial hardships, the Welsh colonists eventually carved out new lives for themselves, and became successful farmers.

'Why do those people wish to move on again, and go to Canada, of all places?' Dada asked.

'Not all of them, Mr Rees,' Bryn replied. 'As I understand it, just a number of them.

'There has been unrest in Patagonia for some time. Their crops have failed and the government of Argentina has passed a law making Spanish the language of instruction in the schools. Also, the young men are required to train in the militia, and the musters are held on the Sabbath day.

'The preservation of the Welsh language and the right to freedom of religion were two of the main reasons for going to Patagonia in the first place. When they decided they would have to leave, there were three choices — America, Palestine or Canada.'

I gave up listening and followed Mam out to the scullery, where she was tackling some pans she had left to soak.

'Poor Gwen,' she said. 'Was this the first you'd heard of this?'

I nodded miserably.

'And you do not want to go to

Canada.' It was a statement, not a question — my mother knew her daughter better than anyone.

'Of course I don't want to go! But what worries me most is the fact that Bryn said nothing to me until now. It should have been discussed before he made his application.'

'What will you do if he gets the job and agrees to go?'

I shook my head again, unable to answer.

'I don't want you to go so far from home,' Mam was saying. 'It's bad enough that the boys are thousands of miles away, without you going, too. But that's the way it is. When a woman marries, she must follow her husband, wherever he chooses to lead her. If you love Bryn, you must be prepared to go with him to Canada.'

My heart was heavy as I realised the truth of her words. But what if I went with Bryn to Canada and we never came home to Wales again? What if I never saw my family again?

Perhaps if I remained firm, Bryn would change his mind.

The sound of the front door closing brought me to my senses and, getting up to look out of the window, I saw Bryn striding off down the street. He had left the house without saying goodbye to me — something which had never happened before.

Sick at heart, I realised all I could do now was to wait, and hope that Bryn would not get the job in Canada.

★ ★ ★

The school, and Cwmbran in general, became a hive of activity as the time of the coronation came near. Strings of bunting appeared all over the town, and mothers were happily looking forward to street parties and planning a mammoth baking spree.

The shops were gaily decorated. Even those which did not sell souvenirs found some way of expressing loyalty to the new monarch. I had to smile when I saw a large picture of the King and Queen perched on the marble slab in the fishmonger's window, surrounded by fish and tastefully decorated with parsley!

The school managers had graciously provided the school with a coronation mug for each child and teacher. I knew that these would not be put to daily use, but would take pride of place on the dressers and mantel shelves of Cwmbran, to be treasured by future generations.

Even the miners were to be given a holiday on the big day, which Mam thought very generous.

Just when coronation fever was at its height, the blow fell. My class were all at assembly one morning towards the end of the school year and Bryn was about to pronounce the benediction when the door opened and one of the older pupils burst in.

'I have a message for the Meistr,' he panted. 'My father said not to wait but to give it at once. It just came by telegraph!'

The boy's father was Evans-the-station, who was usually the first one to learn of any news of the outside world, whether it came over the wire or in the newspapers, which travelled to Cwmbran by train.

'Yes, boy, what is it?' Bryn asked.

'The King is ill, Mr Edwards, and my father says the coronation is off.'

Everyone gasped, but it wasn't until later in the day that we found out that King Edward had appendicitis and was dangerously ill.

The whole village seemed to fall silent as we waited for news.

★ ★ ★

That evening, when we heard the bells of All Saints' Church ring, Mam heaved a sigh of relief.

'Only the usual come-to-meeting chimes. I was expecting them to toll his passing — one stroke for each year of his age.'

'I suppose they want people to go to

the church to pray for the King,' I replied. 'Should we go down to the chapel, Mam?' I knew what she would say.

'Yes, *fach*, just let me get my hat.'

All Saints' Church had only a small congregation, made up mainly of people like the Morgans, who were Church of Wales. Most of the population of Cwmbran were chapel-worshipping under the guidance of Reverend Mr Parry.

We joined in the solemn prayers for the King's recovery, and Mam whispered to me that she was sending up a prayer for the poor Queen as well. I guessed that she was thinking about Dada and how she would feel if he were at death's door.

It seemed that all the people were genuinely sorrowful at this turn of events.

Life is full of perils, I realised suddenly, and I knew I would be devastated if anything happened to Bryn. It was clear to me then that I would follow him to the ends of the earth if necessary.

After the prayers, I looked across the churchyard to where he was chatting to some of the other men and made up my mind.

'I've thought about it,' I said when he broke free of the conversation and approached me, 'and I will come to Canada with you.'

With half of Cwmbran looking on he could do no more than press my hand. But the look in his eyes said it all.

I had committed myself. For better or for worse . . .

★　★　★

The King recovered and the coronation was eventually held on August the ninth.

Although the school year had officially ended, we had a celebratory sports day where the children competed in the usual races and were thrilled to receive penny bars of chocolate as prizes. At the end of the day, one of the governors handed out the promised coronation mugs and the children went home in a state of great contentment.

Our wedding was set for the end of the month, the day before our departure for Canada. Bryn had booked passage for ourselves and Gareth, and we would all travel together.

We were to go by train from Cwmbran up to Liverpool, where we would catch the boat. The sea voyage would take a week or so, and after disembarking at Quebec, we would board a train for the west, travelling on one of the colonist cars about which we had heard so much.

'The train passes quite close to Bangor, where we are going,' Bryn explained. 'Gareth will stay on board to go across Alberta to where Davey is.'

At home, we were in a turmoil trying to decide what would go into my trunk. Saskatchewan was supposed to be very cold in the winter, with deep snow.

'There's a pity, it is, that women cannot wear trousers,' Mam said, with a worried frown. 'Thick stockings you will need, my girl, and red flannel petticoats, and a new pair of boots. And I am going to make you a new serge skirt.'

*   *   *

As the summer sun shone down on Cwmbran, a harsh Saskatchewan winter seemed very far away. I often went for solitary walks, quietly saying goodbye to the land I loved. Even the dirty old buildings in the High Street suddenly seemed precious, for I should not see them again.

I walked by the river, where the yellow musk grew. Despite its name, this flower has no scent, but I had always delighted in finding it. An old man passed me, carrying a coracle on his back and nodding a greeting.

Years ago, Dilys and I had found one of these small, round craft drawn up on the river bank and, greatly daring, had climbed in and attempted to take a ride. Far from going in a straight line, the coracle had spun around in circles! We'd managed to scramble out, but had not dared to speak of our adventure at home.

I must make it up with Dilys now that I was going so far away, I decided. It had been a silly quarrel anyway, for why should she have accepted my brother's proposal of marriage when she did not love him?

There was to be a big gathering at our house before the three of us left for Canada. We would be married in the morning and the party would be in the evening. Then we would take the night train from Cwmbran.

The guests would be mostly friends of Gareth from the colliery and their wives. Dilys and Miss Williams would be there from school, and some of the neighbours would come, including the Roberts family from next door.

Neither of us had many family members who could attend. Bryn's parents were dead, as were my grandparents.

Olwen would come home from Swansea and Mari was to be discharged from the convalescent hospital at last.

My brother Davey would be the only one missing, but I was cheered by the fact that I might see him again in the not too distant future.

★   ★   ★

I had been down in the town, making some last-minute purchases, and was trudging home when our neighbour, Megan Roberts, flew out of our front door, waving urgently.

'Gwen!' she called. 'Thank goodness you've come! It's your mam! She's had a fall and can't get up. I've sent the Richards boy to fetch the doctor.'

Mam was lying on the kitchen floor, obviously in some pain. She had slipped and fallen while reaching up to the top shelf of the dresser.

'Standing on the stool in my stocking feet, I was,' she explained. 'Didn't want to dirty the wood with my shoes.'

I put a cushion under her head and raced upstairs for a blanket to cover her. Then I busied myself picking up broken pieces of china.

It seemed a long time, but I don't suppose it was more than a few minutes before the doctor arrived.

'What's this, then, Mrs Rees? Lying down in the middle of the day, is it, with all this work to be done?' he joked gently. 'That's not like you at all.'

He bent over and gently began to examine her and she winced when he touched her right wrist, which she had been gingerly supporting with the other hand.

'It's the cottage hospital for you, Mrs Rees!' he proclaimed. 'As soon as I get home I'll telephone for an ambulance.'

'Na, na, doctor!' Mam protested. 'I can't go to hospital now, when there's so much to do. My daughter is being married this week and then going to Canada!'

'So I have heard,' the doctor said. 'But I'm afraid you've no choice in the matter, Mrs Rees. You have a broken wrist and possibly some broken ribs. And that bump on the head could be a concussion.

'Miss Rees.' The doctor turned to me. 'Pack a few things for your mother. A nightdress and slippers, and some toilet articles. She will be in the hospital for some time, I'm afraid.'

'But surely they can patch me up and let me come home again?' Mam cried, but he did not answer.

'Should I send for Dada, Doctor?' I asked. 'He is down the pit today.'

'No, Miss Rees, there is no point in bringing the man from his work. There's nothing he can do here.'

He could comfort Mam, I wanted to say, but the gruff words made sense. She would be on her way to the hospital before Dada could be reached below ground, and he could ill afford to lose a day's pay if there were hospital bills to come.

So Mam was loaded into the ambulance while I stood dolefully at the front door. The driver was kindly and the horse seemed placid enough, so perhaps the jolting would not be too bad.

It was unfortunate that the accident had happened on a weekday, as visitors were only allowed on Sunday afternoons. Dada was very upset, and after taking his bath and bolting his meal, he got ready to go out again.

'There's no point in going to the hospital, they won't let you see Mam.'

'I am going to the surgery,' he told me. 'You have already explained things to me, but I want to hear it for myself. The doctor might say more to me, being the husband.'

'This could not have come at a worse time, Gwen,' Gareth said to me after Dada had gone. 'With the two of us about to leave for Canada.'

'No, indeed,' I agreed. 'How long will they keep Mam in the hospital, I wonder?'

When Dada came back his face was grave.

'They will keep your mother in the hospital for a few days,' he explained. 'She has a mild concussion. They have strapped up the broken ribs and are putting her wrist in plaster.'

'Poor Mam!'

'Yes, indeed, and I shall have to make some arrangements here before I go to see her on Sunday. The last thing she needs is to be worrying over what is happening at home.'

'I'll do everything I can, Dada.'

'I know that, *cariad*, but you are leaving for Canada soon. I'll be all right here on my own — it's after your mam comes home that the need will be greatest. Olwen will have to come home,' he finished firmly.

'She'll not like that!' I told him.

'Probably not, but there's no other choice. It is Olwen's duty to come — surely any daughter would do that for her mother?'

But Dada was wrong.

Olwen came home as planned for the wedding, bringing Mari with her. My little sister seemed to have grown two inches while she was convalescing, but although the roses were back in her cheeks, she wore a serious expression which had never been there before. Her illness had affected her a lot.

Dada did not mention our dilemma until Mari was safely in bed.

'You had better go back to Swansea tomorrow and ask for time off to nurse your mother,' he told Olwen.

'I'm sorry, Dada.' Olwen's face hardened. 'I can't do that.'

'Cannot, or will not?' Dada asked, trying to control his temper.

'I'm doing well in my job. If I lose my place I'll be back where I started,' Olwen pointed out.

'Surely they would keep your place open for you?'

'I cannot count on that. There are others waiting to step into my shoes.' Olwen shook her head. 'No, Dada. I am sorry for Mam, and I will send money to help pay for a woman to come to help, but that is all I can do.'

My father and Olwen were glaring at each other like two cats spoiling for a fight. If Mam could have seen them she would have been greatly distressed.

'You will do as you are told!' Dada thundered. ' 'Honour thy father and thy mother', the Bible says. When parents are in need it is the unmarried daughter who must come to help them.'

'There is more than one unmarried daughter here,' Olwen told him, facing him with her arms folded.

'Not for long! Gwen will be married soon and Mari is too young to be depended on.'

Olwen said nothing as Dada reached for his cap and stormed out of the house.

'It will only be for a few weeks,' I pleaded. 'Then you will be able to go back to Swansea, if that is what you want.'

'What I want, Gwen Rees, is to have some sort of life while I am young enough to enjoy it,' Olwen told me. 'When I get married I'll be expected to work in the house until I'm old and grey. You've had an interesting job and now you're off to travel the world. Why do you have all the luck, while they expect me to be a drudge?'

I was so taken aback I could hardly think straight. The silence hung heavy between us.

When Dada came home, he again tried to take a firm hand with Olwen. But once again they began to quarrel. In the end, Olwen flew upstairs and packed her wicker case — and then she was gone, slamming the door behind her.

Dada and I looked at each other. No words were spoken, but we both knew there was only one solution left to us.

For the time being, I'd be staying at home.

Heartache

Life settled down into a routine with Bryn and Gareth gone, and at Cwmbran School, the new term had started without me.

A new teacher had taken my place in the infants' room, and there was a new headmaster.

'I don't like the new Meistr,' Mari confided. 'He never tells us interesting stories like Mr Edwards, and he's always making a fuss about nothing.'

'That old Protheroe!' Dilys agreed. 'Just like being in the army, it is. Every request for something from the stock cupboard has to be put in writing.

'And he's far too interfering, always asking us if we go to chapel. Got to set a good example to the children, he says. Go to chapel, indeed! And me a minister's daughter.'

'It sounds as if your father will like

him,' I said wickedly. 'He'll be wanting the pair of you to marry next, since our Gareth was such a disappointment.'

'Some hopes!' Dilys laughed. 'If I manage to get through the term without being rude to Mr Protheroe it will be an accomplishment in itself, never mind marriage!'

Secretly I was glad that the new headmaster was proving so unpopular. I had no wish for Bryn to be forgotten by the pupils he had cared about so much.

I wondered how he was getting on in Canada, for I had heard nothing. Every day I waited for Jenkins the post, only to be disappointed as he trudged past our door. Then I had to get through the day somehow until he came round again the next morning.

Gareth wrote and told us that he had gone west by train, leaving Bryn in Saskatchewan. Gareth had gone to the far side of Alberta to a region known as the Crowsnest Pass, where Davey had met him.

There is quite a little village here, he

had written. *Wooden houses are inhabited by the miners and their families. Davey and I share with two other men.*

Because I have been hired as a tunneller I work the day shift all the time, and I have another man to assist me. The pay is good because it is skilled work.

And you'll never guess who we met on the ship coming out — Verity's aunt, Mrs Euphemia Forbes! At the Sunday service we Welshmen led the singing. Afterwards, a lady came up to congratulate us on our voices and asked where we were from. When we told her Cwmbran, she asked if we knew the Morgans.

'My nephew owns the colliery there,' she said.

I knew what was coming next. She told us her nephew's daughter had run off to Canada with a miner and was now working as a housemaid. Of course, she had to be brought back.

Davey sent a wire to Verity and she managed to get away before Miss

Forbes caught up with her. She is here now, staying with a married couple. Davey will ask the circuit preacher to marry them when he next comes through.

★ ★ ★

Unable to do any work around the house, Mam recovered quickly.

'Like a little holiday this is,' she enthused. 'I could quite enjoy sitting here like the lady of the manor, watching someone else do the work. Makes me feel like Mrs Morgan up at the House.'

When she was able to walk about, she took to going next door to visit Mamgu, our elderly neighbour.

'It means I can get out with Gwilym more often,' Megan told me. 'To tell you the truth, Gwen, he is getting impatient, having to wait so long for us to get married.'

'Lots of people stay engaged for years while they save up to get married,' I

211

replied — but that was the wrong thing to say.

'Yes, indeed, but not a penny have I made, staying home here all this time. It's not like you, up at the school.'

'Not any more, Megan.'

'Then you know how it feels,' she replied. 'It takes all of my brother Llew's pay to keep us here. I'll have nothing to contribute when Gwilym and I do get wed — if we ever do.'

'Doesn't your sister Gladys help out?'

'From time to time, yes, but she will need the money herself now that she is engaged as well.'

'Gladys is engaged?' I asked, amazed.

'Oh, yes. To an under-gardener at the House,' she explained. 'Getting married at Christmas, they are, and they'll have a room over the stables.'

I was happy for Gladys, but I couldn't help feeling sad. Four thousand miles separated me from the man I loved and Megan was worried that her own engagement might come to nothing, too.

'I'm afraid he'll find someone else if I don't look out,' Megan confided, a worried frown creasing her brow. 'That's why I am glad to have your mam sit with Mamgu. She can always bang on the wall if anything goes wrong, because you'll always be right next door.'

Yes, I thought, and unfortunately next door to Megan's brother, Llew. He had always had a soft spot for me, and now, with Bryn gone, he began to pay me even more attention. He was always there, ready to help or offering to do little jobs.

When he was on the day-shift, he started coming over to the house to visit Dada, sitting at the table, debating some political or historical argument. I could see that Dada enjoyed the company.

'I wish he wouldn't come so often,' I muttered to Mam, who looked at me in surprise.

'Your father likes his company, *cariad*. And it is good for a fatherless young man to have an older man to look up to. He will always be welcome in this house.'

There was no answer to that. Llew's mother had been a very good friend of Mam's, and was greatly missed.

'Very nice manners, he has,' Mam went on.

'I suppose you would like me to marry Llew and live next door!' I blurted out.

'Na, na, *cariad*,' Mam soothed. 'You will marry your Bryn, and that is good. But I can't deny I would like to have you living next door to me rather than going far away to Canada.'

If there was any justice in the world, Bryn would be next door, I thought dejectedly, and Llew would be in Canada. But life, I was learning, is seldom fair.

★ ★ ★

Shortly before the school broke up for the Christmas holidays, I received a letter, obviously posted in Cwmbran. I had been lurking by the front door as usual, waiting for the postman, hoping for a letter from Bryn.

Disappointed, I pushed the envelope into my apron pocket and went back to the housework.

It was only when I was sitting down with Mam for our mid-morning cup of tea that I remembered the letter and read it.

'It's from the new headmaster, Mr Evan Protheroe,' I told Mam, 'He is asking me to go to the school tomorrow, to meet with the staff. I wonder why?'

'Perhaps they want to invite you to the Christmas concert, to see your old scholars perform.' Mam suggested.

'If that was the case, why not simply say so in the letter?'

Intrigued, I went to the school the following day. It gladdened my heart to hear the greetings of the children as they shot past me on their way home. It brought it home to me how much I had missed their bright little faces.

I found the staff in Miss Williams' room perched uncomfortably on long desks. A pale, quiet-looking young woman was introduced as my replacement, Miss Lilian John. The only man present was obviously the new headmaster, Evan Protheroe.

'You must be Miss Rees.' Evan Protheroe, a short, balding man, extended a hand before Dilys had a chance to introduce us. 'I will not beat about the bush. I want to know if you would be interested in coming back here to teach after the holidays.'

This was not what I had expected. I looked round to see Dilys beaming encouragement.

'I am leaving Cwmbran School, Miss Rees,' Miss Williams' explained. 'I was intending to retire at the end of the school year but my arthritis is so bad that my doctor advises me to go now.' Her voice was low and she looked sad. My heart went out to her.

'I am very sorry to hear that, Miss

Williams,' I said genuinely.

Miss Williams and I may not always have seen eye to eye, but I could not deny her talent for teaching. She had given many faithful years to the school and would be sorely missed, by parents and pupils alike.

'Would I be teaching the infants again?' I asked Mr Protheroe cautiously.

'No, you would be in charge of the top classes, in place of Miss Williams,' he explained. 'She assures me you are equal to the task. The only alternative would be to transfer Miss John there, and that would not do.'

In one breath Mr Protheroe had managed to insult both the new teacher and myself. I could see he would not be the easiest person to work with and I vowed not to make it too easy for him to lure me back.

'I shall discuss your offer with my parents and let you know as soon as possible,' I replied.

'I'll look forward to hearing from you,' he said abruptly, before turning away and disappearing into the tiny office which had been Bryn's.

'Oh, you must come back, Gwen,' Dilys enthused as we walked home. 'It hasn't been the same without you.'

'Of course I'm coming back!' I told Dilys, laughing. 'I'm walking on air at the thought. I've missed the children so much and now I can start saving the fare to Canada. Oh, Dilys, you don't know what this means to me!'

'Then why were you so evasive with Mr Protheroe?' she asked.

'Didn't want to seem too eager, did I?' I laughed. 'I have to start as I mean to go on.'

Mam was delighted when I gave her my news.

'There's glad, I am, Gwen. I was so sorry when you had to give up everything to look after me. You go back to the school. I'm sure I can manage now.'

'You still can't do any heavy lifting,' I reminded her, but she dismissed this with a smile.

'You'll still have to do the washing and scrubbing, *fach*, but I can manage the cooking and sweeping now.'

'I'm sure that Llew will help — if you ask him — to carry water and bring in the coal!' I laughed. 'He is round here every minute; we may as well put him to work.'

I was joking, of course, but something else occurred to me then. I would get Dilys to call in more often to discuss lesson plans and she could tell me about the children and their individual needs. She had always harboured romantic feelings for Llew, and since he was now spending so much time at our house, perhaps . . . in time . . .

Christmas brought a fat bundle of letters from Bryn. I was overjoyed.

You will think I have forgotten you, he wrote, *but I have not had the opportunity to post anything until now.*

This western country is made up of huge, empty tracts of land and there is no way to get from one place to another

*except by walking. Even then, I should
not know which way to go.*

*The father of one of my pupils has a
horse and wagon. He is going to the
nearest town before winter sets in, and
has promised to take me with him to
buy supplies.*

I tried to imagine Bryn being jolted
across the prairie with his new friend
and wondered if they spoke English at
the shop! I understood that western
Canada was full of immigrants from
many nations.

It felt as though we were living in
completely different worlds.

The schools are very different here,
Bryn continued. *They are basically just
one large room filled with benches. The
teacher has to instruct children of all
ages. There are no Welsh textbooks, so
reading must be taught with the help of
the Bible.*

Strange, I thought, when they had
advertised for a teacher of Welsh. I
supposed there was not much money
for books.

They have a strange system called 'boarding round'. I was told that I would be staying in the home of each pupil for a month at a time, before moving on to the next. Not my idea of a settled home life, I can tell you, especially as the houses are quite spartan.

My school has a loft upstairs, and I persuaded the trustees to put a bed up there for me. After much grumbling, they agreed, so I sleep there and do my cooking on the wood stove downstairs.

In my mind's eye, I pictured Bryn getting up on a cold morning, coming down a ladder and making breakfast in the schoolroom!

There's lonely without you, I am, cariad. I live for the day when we shall be married.

Davey will be happy at last, now that his Verity has gone to join him. I can't decide whether it is better for you to come to Canada next summer, as we had planned, or for me to return to Wales when my contract is up.

Write and tell me what you think.

221

★ ★ ★

Olwen came home for Christmas, and received a welcome similar to that given the prodigal son in the Bible. Now that the crisis was over, Dada was prepared to forgive her.

She kept us all entertained with funny stories about her work at the hotel, including one about an old lady who wanted to know if she could have a discount if she brought her own bed linen! She certainly seemed to be meeting all sorts of unusual characters in her new life.

I did notice that someone called 'Vic' began to crop up more and more in her stories.

'Who's this Vic?' I asked at last.

Olwen went red and tossed her head. 'Just a friend.'

'A special friend? You seem to mention him rather a lot.' I took care to speak mildly. I didn't want her flouncing off in one of her fits of pique until Christmas was safely past.

'He's someone who stays at the hotel, a commercial traveller.' She looked over her shoulder to make sure nobody was listening, then she felt inside the neck of her blouse and pulled out a pretty locket. 'He gave me this, for Christmas.'

'Very nice,' I told her.

I was curious to know if there was a picture of the young man inside, but I didn't dare ask. After all, it was only natural at her age that she should have a young man. She must know Vic quite well if she felt able to accept an expensive gift . . .

*　*　*

At Easter, Mam suggested that I go to Swansea to stay with Olwen for a few days.

'Do you good, a bit of sea air, Gwen,' she told me.

The idea appealed to me — I didn't often get to the seaside. So off I went, Olwen having assured me that I'd be allowed to share her room at no charge.

It wasn't long before I met Vic, and I could quite see why Olwen liked him. Tall and dapper, with dark hair and smiling eyes, he could have posed for an illustration in a story paper. He wasn't Bryn, of course, but he was pleasant enough.

It did occur to me, however, that he spent most of the time talking about himself and I could see that Olwen hung on his every word.

'So, what did you think?' she asked after Vic had gone.

'He seems very nice,' I replied carefully. 'I suppose the next step will be to introduce him to Mam and Dada?'

Olwen looked away — rather too quickly for my liking. Alarm bells began to ring in my mind.

'Olwen!' I said. 'Is there something you haven't told me?'

She hesitated. 'The thing is, Gwen, he's — he's married.'

She hurried on, explaining that his marriage had been over for a long time and that his wife didn't understand him.

I groaned.

'We love each other, Gwen!' she went on dramatically. 'Surely you of all people can understand?'

'I can't imagine what Dada will say when he hears this,' I remarked, although I had a pretty good idea.

'Oh, you mustn't tell him, Gwen. Promise you won't!' Olwen pleaded. 'They'll make me come home, and if I can't see Vic again I'll die. I'll just die!'

Reluctantly I gave my word, knowing how heartbroken I had been when circumstances had separated me from Bryn.

*   *   *

When I reached home, nursing my guilty secret. I noticed that my father was sitting quietly in his chair.

'Anything wrong, Dada?' I asked when he did not return my greeting.

There was no reply and Mam looked

at him in alarm.

'Huw, *cariad*, what is the matter?' she asked. 'Tell us.'

'Come and sit down,' he said, sighing. 'You, too, Gwen.'

'You might as well know,' he began as we both hurriedly obeyed. 'You will see it in the newspaper in any case. There's been a terrible disaster in Canada. At a mine in the Crowsnest area . . . ' He gestured to the paper lying open on the table.

My heart plummeted and Mam went as white as snow.

'But that is where Gareth and Davey are!' she cried. 'It must be bad if they've printed the story over here in Wales — thousands of miles away.'

I read the story with growing horror. The disaster was at a place called Frank, a community built by a mining company. At four o'clock in the morning there had been a terrible landslide, when a huge rock mass had broken away from nearby Turtle Mountain.

226

Limestone rock had poured down over the little community, wiping out the town and covering the mine itself. Much of the nearby railway had also been destroyed.

'There is more than one mine in the Crowsnest area,' I said. 'Perhaps the boys are nowhere near this place.'

In our misery, none of us could remember the name of the mine where Gareth and Davey were working. Mam went upstairs to retrieve the treasured bundle of letters from her bureau.

'It doesn't say where they are,' she said at last, trying to hold back the tears. 'Davey mentioned the name of the mining company, but that is all.'

She read through the letters again, as if the longed-for information would miraculously appear.

*   *   *

The next day we waited anxiously for the newspapers to appear in the shops, hoping for more information. Dada even visited the manager's office when he went to work, in the vain hope that somehow word would have been cabled there from Canada.

The paper reprinted stories from some of the Canadian papers, and the news was grim. Millions of tons of rock had fallen on the little town. There was no hope of rescuing those trapped, although a few had escaped the onslaught.

One man described being awakened by a noise which he had thought was an explosion in the mine. He rushed outside and saw the mountain sliding past him, within four-hundred yards of his door!

Railway workers on a siding heard rocks breaking away from the mountain, and the engineer was able to get up steam and move the train out of harm's way.

But nothing was known of the miners on the night-shift . . .

We could only hope and pray that our Gareth and Davey had not been among them.

The Waiting Is Over

At long last the newspaper had the information we had been waiting and praying for. Dada rushed into the house, jubilantly waving a copy above his head.

No Welshmen Dead In Canadian Mine Disaster, the headline reported.

'It says here that they are calling in doctors to see what they can do to help the survivors,' Dada told us. 'And they're bringing in men of the North West Mounted Police to supervise the area. There may still be the danger of landslide.'

'This has been the longest few days of my life,' Mam put in. 'And it's not over yet — not until we hear from Gareth and Davey themselves will I believe that they're truly safe.'

As if in answer to Mam's request, a letter from Gareth arrived a few days later.

'You read it to me, *fach*,' Mam said, handing me the pages. 'I'm all of a dither.'

''Have you heard about the disaster here in Alberta?'' I read aloud. ''A mountain collapsed on the coal mine at Frank, leaving tons of rock on the village below. It is miles from where Davey and I are working at present, but we went on the rescue train to see if we could help. I cannot describe how terrible it was to see the place.

''There were men down the mine when the mountain collapsed, but some of them managed to tunnel their way out. People are calling it a miracle.''

'But the newspapers are saying that millions of tons of rock have come down,' Mam protested. 'How could they make their way through all that?'

''Only about twenty men were down below that night, checking the timbers,'' I read on. ''A Welshman, Joe Chapman, was the foreman. He's given a statement saying that at four o'clock, the coal began to break up around him.

The men were alarmed and headed for the ladders but found their way blocked by fallen rock. They went back and tried another tunnel, but it was flooded.

''I suppose they thought it was an ordinary cave-in and the rescue crews would soon be searching for them. If they had known there was millions of tons of rock above them, they might have given way to despair.''

Mam was listening to this with wide eyes and I saw that Mari was chewing on the end of one plait, a habit I'd thought she'd outgrown.

''The foreman knew that a certain seam of coal came out on the mountain some way back and they decided to try to tunnel their way out in that direction,'' I read. ''The men worked in relays, singing to keep their spirits up.

''Finally, when they had almost given up hope, a man gave one last despairing swing of his pick and a rush of cold air blew in on them. Before long, they had enlarged the hole and emerged into the outside world.''

'It was a miracle,' Mam breathed.

'Yes,' I agreed, pausing from my reading to take in all this news.

'And to know that our boys are safe and well,' she continued, looking very much relieved, 'is a great weight from my shoulders.'

I was saying a thankful prayer to myself as I prepared for school a little later when there was a knock at the front door.

'Can I come in?' Megan said urgently as soon as I opened the door.

It was obvious from the strained look on her face that something was wrong.

She followed me into the kitchen where Mam looked up at her with surprise. It was unlike Megan to come calling so early in the day.

'Hello, Megan,' Mam said. 'Everything all right, is it?'

'Na, na, it isn't,' Megan said, a tear running down her cheek. 'It's Mamgu, Mrs Rees. She's dead.'

'Dead!' Mam cried. 'Here, sit down, child, while Gwen pours you a nice cup of tea. Still plenty in the pot, there is.'

Megan explained what had happened in between sips of hot tea.

'I overslept this morning and Llew must have gone out without looking in on Mamgu,' she began. 'No reason why he should, really. I'm the one who looks after her in the morning.

'I wondered why she hadn't called out to me or thumped on the ceiling with her stick, but I found her when I took her tea in to her. She was lying there, all peaceful.'

'What a shock for you,' I said.

'Would you like me to come round and help lay her out, *cariad*?' Mam asked, but Megan shook her head.

'I went next door to Mrs Lewis and she is sending for the doctor, and I've been to see Mrs Thomas from Lister Street.'

Mrs Thomas was a miner's wife who helped to support their ten children by acting as midwife in the district. She could also be relied upon to lay out the departed.

'Llew doesn't know yet, of course,' Megan continued. 'And someone will have to go up to the House to tell Gladys. Compassionate leave she will have to have, for the funeral if nothing else.

She looked down at her lap and smoothed her green skirt with a look of distaste. 'I have nothing to wear for mourning.'

'I can help with that,' Mam told her. 'Go down to Evans the draper this morning and buy some black stuff for a dress and skirt.'

'Thank you, Mrs Rees,' Megan said, before the tears began to flow in earnest.

'I was so unkind to her last night!' she sobbed. 'You know how she used to say, 'Well, that's another meal closer the grave'? It used to irritate me so much so, and finally I snapped.

''Why do you have to keep saying that, Mamgu?' I shouted at her. Just think, that was the last thing I ever said to her! Harsh words, and now she is gone and no chance to say sorry.'

'Megan, *cariad*, we all get tired and cross at times, and say things we do not mean.' Mam knew exactly what to say. 'Your grandmother would have understood that. All these years you have cared for her so faithfully and I know that she was grateful. Many a time she told me that she did not know where she would be without you.'

After school that afternoon, I went round to see what I could do to help Megan. She handed me a framed photo which I had often seen before but never examined closely.

'That's Mamgu and Tadcu just after they were married,' she told me. 'I'll have it up in my room now, beside the one I have of Mam and Dad.'

'She was very pretty in her youth,' I said. 'And your grandfather was a good-looking man, too. Llew takes after him, don't you think?'

The young bridegroom was seated on a chair with his legs crossed and his pretty bride was standing behind him with one hand on his shoulder. Neither one was smiling, as was the photographic custom of the day.

'Mamgu told me they each had their heads in a clamp,' Megan told me, 'although you can't see it in the picture.'

'Really?' I asked, amazed.

Megan shrugged. 'Something about not moving and blurring the picture. Anyway, I have to get this parlour in order before the funeral. It's good of you to help, Gwen.'

'It's no trouble,' I said. After everything she'd done for Mamgu, I thought, Megan certainly deserved all the help she was being given by friends and neighbours.

The day finally came when Mamgu was taken to her last resting place, to lie beside her husband. Dada and Llew went to the funeral, of course, walking behind the horse-drawn hearse with its black trappings.

But Mam and I and the other women waited next door with Megan and

Gladys, ready to serve the mourners with the 'funeral baked meats' when they returned. Women in Cwmbran did not attend funerals.

* * *

Summer came, with warm rains alternating with long, bright days when the sun shone until late in the evening. Mari complained bitterly about being sent to bed at nine o'clock while the joyful shouts of more fortunate children at play could be heard through the open windows.

'It is not long since you were a patient in that convalescent home, child,' Mam said determinedly. 'We have to take care — or it's outgrowing your strength you'll be.'

When I went upstairs, I found Mari leaning out of the open window, gazing at one of her schoolmates in the street below who was making rude faces at her.

'You won't tell Mam, will you,

Gwen?' she asked, turning from the window.

'Tell Mam about Enid pulling funny faces?' I teased. 'Come on, back into bed with you.'

'Nobody can sleep in daylight,' she complained.

'Then get into bed and look at your library book.'

'I don't feel like doing that either.' She slipped under the covers and sat hugging her knees. 'Tell me about the weddings that are going to happen instead. Everybody is getting married — you, Olwen, Gladys and Megan.' She looked at me hopefully. 'There's lovely to be a bridesmaid, Gwen.'

'Nobody is getting married just yet,' I told her. 'Now lie down, Mari *fach*, and let me tuck you in.'

This time she did as she was told and, having seen her snuggled down, I went to the window myself, drinking in the warm night air.

Here we were, four brides-in-waiting. Dear Megan was free to marry her

Gwilym at last, although the happy day had had to be postponed yet again now that she was in mourning.

Gladys was in the same boat, of course, so the sisters planned a double wedding when the year of observance was up.

'A very quiet occasion it will be,' Megan had told me. 'Just the four of us — me and Gwilym, Gladys and Frederick. We'll be witnesses for each other, and then back home and have a few close friends in for a meal.

'How about you and Olwen — will that be a double wedding, too?'

'Not likely,' I said gloomily. 'No chance of a wedding for me, with the bridegroom four thousand miles away.'

And, I added to myself, Olwen's beau already has a wife! What a hopeless pair of brides-to-be we are!

'Everything comes to those who wait,' Megan said, trying to comfort me. 'I thought my day would never come, but look, here we are!'

★　　★　　★

I was finding it increasingly hard to keep Olwen's secret. But, out of the blue, matters came to a head.

It was the wettest day we had had in a long time. The rain was pounding down on the pavements, flooding the gutters and gurgling into drains. It was a good day to stay indoors and do some useful work.

I was ironing, tackling a huge pile of sheets and pillowcases. There were four flat irons on the go, one in my hand and the other three heating on the hob. The kitchen was festooned with freshly-ironed shirts and blouses, for I had vowed to get the whole job done in one fell swoop.

Mam was sitting at the table, reading a letter from the boys. Knowing her love of flowers, Gareth had taken pains to describe the many beautiful plants which grew wild in the Canadian West.

''After the winter, it almost seems like a miracle that these flowers have survived,'' she read aloud. ''Several feet of snow have covered the earth for months.

''Tell Gwen that Davey and I are sending her a surprise packet. It should arrive any day now,'' she finished.

'Whatever can it be?' Dada asked, standing at her shoulder to see the letter for himself.

'I don't know. Some souvenir of Canada, I suppose,' Mam mused. 'Something for the girl's bottom drawer.'

I smiled; it was kind of my brothers to think of me, I thought.

Just then, there was a frenzied rapping at the front door. Mam struggled to her feet.

Absorbed in my work, I barely listened to the muted voices outside, although whoever had come calling did not sound Welsh. I was surprised when Mam came back to the kitchen with a bedraggled-looking woman in tow.

'Sit by the fire,' Mam said, indicating a chair and moving the clothes-horse to a safer location. 'Hand me your cape and take off your hat. Dripping all over the floor, you are.'

'Now, Mrs Harris,' Mam continued when they were both settled, 'you had better tell us what this is about.'

Not much of a welcome, I thought. It wasn't like Mam at all. There was no offer of tea and the visitor seemed uncomfortable.

There was silence for a while and I carried on ironing, glad of something to do.

The woman spoke up at last. 'I had to come, Mrs Rees. What would you have done in my place?'

Slowly the story came out. She lived in Manchester and was married to a Welshman, Vic Harris. My head shot up at this. Not Olwen's Vic!

'He is a commercial traveller,' she explained, 'and often away from home. I am used to that, but recently he has been staying away for longer periods.

'This time he has stayed away for almost three weeks, and I am beside myself with worry. I knew he was in

Wales because he sent a picture postcard to our little boy.'

'You have a little boy?' I stammered.

The woman turned to look at me.

'That's right. Tom, his name is. I have a little girl, too — Mavis. She's just over a year now, and starting to toddle.'

Oh, Olwen, I thought. What have you done?

'The rent is due and I was running out of money,' the woman continued. 'I was at the end of my tether, so I thought I would come and see what Vic was up to. Swansea, the postmark said, so I left the children with my neighbour and made my way here.'

'But Swansea is a big place,' Mam said. 'How did you know where to find him?'

'I did the rounds of all the hotels and boarding-houses until I came to the Red Dragon,' she said simply. 'I asked the girl at the reception desk if she had a Mr Vic Harris staying there and she said no, not at present, but his fiancée, Miss Olwen Rees, worked there and would know where to find him.

'I told a lie then, and said there had been a death in the family. The receptionist said Olwen's family was in Cwmbran. So I caught a train, and here I am.'

'We have not seen Olwen for some time,' Mam told her. 'I understand that she does know a man called Vic, but there is certainly no engagement.'

'No, there couldn't be, could there, Mrs Rees?' The poor woman was bewildered. 'Vic is married already.'

She dipped into her shabby handbag and pulled out a studio photograph of herself, sitting in a chair with a baby on her lap and a little boy holding a small wooden horse on wheels. Standing proudly behind the little family was a dapper young man — Vic!

'I know that the receptionist must be mistaken,' Mam said curtly. 'Olwen is inclined to be foolish, yes. But she is not bad.

'There's sorry I am that you have come all this way for nothing.'

Mam then made an offer of tea, which the woman gratefully accepted. Then, putting on her damp garments, she left our house, not telling us where she was going or how she was going to manage. She cut a sad figure, wending her weary way down the street.

'I feel we should have given her a bed for the night, Gwen,' Mam said with tears in her eyes. 'But — and I'm sorry to say it — I just wanted her out of the house. You were in Swansea . . . Do you know if there is any truth in this?'

I felt awful, seeing Mam looking so miserably at me, but I couldn't bring myself to tell her anything. It was Olwen's doing and I felt it was up to her to explain. I only hoped it was not too late to put a stop to the whole sorry affair.

★   ★   ★

Lately I'd heard from Bryn more often. In his last letter, he'd written of how he had decided to return to Wales when his year of teaching was up.

The original plan — which had been for me to join him in Canada when Mam recovered from her injuries — had fallen by the wayside after he had discovered what conditions were like over there. The winters lasted for six months or more, and Bryn had shivered in his sleeping quarters under the rafters until he'd finally given in and moved his bed downstairs to the classroom, close to the stove.

It made my heart ache to think of him being so uncomfortable.

'There's funny it sounds.' Dilys giggled, when I recounted this tale to her. 'Can you imagine what our pupils would say if they found Mr Protheroe stretched out on a mattress in Cwmbran School?'

'I don't think the people in Canada would see it in the same way,' I remarked. 'Bryn has written of children struggling through waist-high snow-drifts to get to school.'

Dilys marvelled at that — it all seemed so foreign to us.

Knowing that our wedding would not be long delayed, I began to make small economies, trying to save as much as possible. Giving up sweets and getting my shoes cobbled instead of buying new ones was a small price to pay for the happiness which was to come.

I sang as I walked to school, and was rewarded with smiles from the people I passed in the street.

As the weeks passed, Megan spent happy hours in our house, where Mam was helping her to make a costume for her wedding.

There was no fairytale gown and veil for her, however.

'When would I ever wear a white frock again?' she asked. 'It's different for the gentry — they can wear their gowns at balls afterwards, I suppose. Anyhow, it's a dark blue costume for me, to wear with a nice white blouse. It will do for chapel later on.'

Each time Gladys had a day off, she came home full of plans, her homely face alight with satisfaction.

She and Frederick were to have the room over the stables for their own little love nest, and it would be furnished with bits and pieces provided by Mrs Morgan.

'And Madam says I can go on working for a time, until I — ' She stopped abruptly as a fiery red blush spread over her features.

'Until your family starts to come,' Mam finished for her. 'There's lucky you are, Gladys. You'll have a little extra money coming in — just as long as Frederick doesn't object to his wife working.'

'Oh, he doesn't care, Mrs Rees. Of course, he's used to seeing me working at the House. Lucky I'm in service, I suppose, not a teacher like Gwen.'

* * *

Each day, I expected to hear from Bryn sending me details of when he planned to return to Wales — and then the blow fell.

Evans the post thrust a letter into my hand, just as I was going down to the town to shop for Mam. Not wanting to go back into the house, I put the envelope in my pocket, thinking it was nice to have something to savour later.

It was not until we had cleared away the dinner things that I had a moment to myself. I told Mam I felt like a walk, and when I was perched on the stile in a field belonging to Penybont Farm, I tore the letter open eagerly.

My face fell when I read what Bryn had to say, however . . .

This will come as a shock to you, cariad, he had written. *I find myself unable to return to Wales at the present time because the school trustees are unable to pay me.*

He went on to explain that the new settlers had little money to spare, having found their expenses in the new country to be higher than they had dreamed.

They have been very good about supplying me with food, and of course I have firewood and accommodation, but it is ready cash that is the problem. So many incomers have to work for years before they have money in their pockets. I know of one teacher who received his year's pay in wheat.

I turned over the page. The next sentence was partly obscured by a large inkblot but I was able to make out enough words to see that Bryn was telling me I should not go out to Canada to join him!

I sat hunched on the stile with what felt like a lead weight in my heart. He had concluded the letter with some tender words which spoke of his love for me, but what good did that do us when we were so far apart? Slowly the tears began to fall . . .

Surprises In Store

Of course, Mam had to tell Dada about our visit from Mrs Harris. As was expected, he was furious.

'A man with a wife and two young children!' he fumed. 'How dare he take advantage of a young girl like Olwen!'

'I'm afraid that Olwen knew quite well what she was up to,' Mam said. 'Gwen has told me everything. Hopelessly in love, they are, so she says.'

'Hopeless is the word for it, Susan! Now you see what comes of reading too many romantic novels. The girl has her head in the air when she needs her feet on the ground.'

'I think she really is in love, Dada,' I ventured.

'Perhaps Olwen believes it, but what about him?' Dad countered. 'He has no business speaking of love to another woman and him not free to do so.'

My parents discussed what they should do about Olwen, including Dad going to Swansea and dragging his daughter home by the ear.

'But you cannot take a day off work, Huw,' Mam told him, and he was forced to agree.

I, too, had my job to go to, and it was a measure of my parents' distress that Mam herself, who hardly ever ventured beyond the door, was prepared to set out for the city.

However, that proved unnecessary. Two days later, the door flew open and a weeping Olwen threw herself into Mam's arms.

'There, there, *cariad*,' Mam soothed, while I looked on. 'Come and sit by the fire and tell me all about it.'

Choking and sobbing, Olwen told her story.

Ruth, a friend from Swansea, had invited her to go to see her married sister in the Rhondda on their days off. This sister had just had a baby which she was eager to show off.

A look of relief came over Mam's face. Olwen had been on a perfectly innocent outing; she had not gone away with Vic!

'But when I got back to work, the other girls couldn't wait to tell me that Vic's wife had been there twice, asking for him. His wife!' She broke into fresh sobs.

'We know, she came here,' I put in.

'I was so mortified, Mam,' she continued. 'I knew all along it couldn't come to anything, me and Vic, but I couldn't help myself. Half of me knew what I should do, and the other half thought that somehow it might all come right.

'While I was away, I talked to my friend Ruth about it, and I made up my mind I had to finish with Vic. But the idea that his wife had actually come looking for him made it all seem so sordid. And now everyone knows how stupid I've been.'

Mam smoothed Olwen's hair as she used to when we were children.

'Vic came back to the hotel,' Olwen went on. 'When I told him his wife had been there, he only laughed. 'She's a foolish woman,' he said. 'I've told you that before, haven't I?' '

' 'Foolish or not,' I said, 'she is your wife, Vic. I have made up my mind that we must not see each other again.' '

'That was good, *cariad*,' Mam told her. 'Upset, was he?'

'Upset?' Olwen held her damp handkerchief to her mouth and gave another sob. 'He said he'd only been seeing me to pass the time while he was away from home. He had never loved me, and there's silly I was to have taken him seriously!

'I believed him! He said he loved me, and he talked about marriage!'

'Ah, Olwen, first love is always painful. But you are young yet,' Mam soothed. 'The right man will come along some day.'

Olwen had taken herself to bed before Dada came home. It was left to Mam to explain.

'There's wicked she is, putting us through all this distress,' he said. 'Whatever will the girl do next? It's too soft with her we've been all these years.'

I understood, of course, that his harsh words were born of worry.

Once, one of my pupils had not arrived home on time and his mother had come hurrying up to the school to see if he had been kept in. When she learned that he was not there, she had become frantic.

I had helped search for the little boy, whom we came across in the street.

He had gone to Penybont Farm to see the new lambs, unaware of the fuss he had caused. In her relief, his loving mother had forgotten her sorrow and given him a good slap on the leg, with promises of more to follow if he ever did such a thing again.

I remembered this now, for I knew that my parents loved Olwen as much as any of us, despite the fact that she was such a trial to us.

Being a child, Mari did not understand this aspect of parenthood.

'Why are you all against her?' She spoke up loyally in Olwen's defence. 'There's kind, she was, when I was in the nursing home. She came to see me every Sunday, always bringing a little treat. When I was better, she took me to the seaside.

'Did she, *fach*?' Dada asked.

'We went on the sands, where we saw a Punch and Judy show, and I had an ice-cream cornet,' Mari continued. 'There were donkey rides, too, but they were only for little children, not meant for people like myself who have ridden ponies.'

'Ay, we all have our good side,' Dada conceded.

'That is all very well, Huw.' Mam put down her sewing. 'Of course Olwen is a good girl, even if she is a bit thoughtless at times. But I want to know that she has learned her lesson and will be more careful in future!'

'Oh, she will learn her lesson, Susan,'

Dada told her determinedly. 'She will not be going back to Swansea for a start. I was a fool ever to agree to it. No more jobs away from home for Miss Olwen Rees for quite some time to come!'

'I doubt if she would want to go back in any case,' Mam told him, stitching away with a little smile on her face.

Her ewe lamb was safely home and, as she remarked to me later, she believed that the storm had passed over, with no lasting damage done.

Olwen's bruised heart would soon mend. She was only eighteen, after all . . .

* * *

A small package was delivered to our house one morning and, glancing at the stamp, Mam brought it to me.

'From Canada,' she said. 'It must be your present from the boys, Gwen.'

'I don't think so, Mam,' I said, laughing. 'Did you not notice? It's addressed to you. Go on, open it.'

She opened it eagerly and let out a gasp when she saw the photograph it contained.

'Look at this, *cariad*, there's wonderful!' she cried, breaking down with happy tears.

There, staring at me from the sepia picture, was my brother Davey, all spruced up and sitting in a fancy carved chair beside a potted palm.

Standing beside him, with one hand possessively on his shoulder, was Verity Morgan — or Verity Rees, as we had to call her now.

You are looking at a picture of the new Mr and Mrs Dafydd Rees, Davey had written. *Verity and I were married on Saturday morning by the Methodist circuit preacher, with Gareth and a friend as witnesses.*

You will be surprised to know that one of the owners of the mine here gave a small reception for us at his home. I had thought it would be a shabby wedding indeed. As you know, Gareth and I are not much good at cooking, and to ask a bride to cook for a crowd on her wedding day would hardly have been right.

But when the owner's wife learned that my bride-to-be was a Morgan from Cwmbran, she said that her husband and Watkin Morgan had been at school together in England years ago, and it was the least they could do to make our wedding a festive occasion.

'There's lovely, Gwen.' Mam smiled. 'And see what he says about this picture.'

The photo was taken later in the day by an itinerant photographer who came in on the train, bringing his 'props' with him. The mining company had hired him to take a group photo of all the men, but he was glad enough to earn a little extra from us.

Three copies, we ordered. One for ourselves, one for you and one for the Morgans.

A letter from Verity will be going to them by the same post.

Verity had also enclosed a note for Mam, in which she apologised for any trouble she might have caused. She felt sure that Mam, as his mother, would understand why she loved Davey so much!

'There's funny it is, Gwen!' Mam laughed. 'Now Dada and I are in-laws with the Morgans! Can you imagine it?' She chuckled.

I grinned. 'Better than out-laws. I wonder what they'll think, though, Mam. They'll probably cast her off without a shilling, if they haven't already done so.'

But it seemed that the Morgans were resigned to the fact that Verity and Davey were actually married . . .

'They seem relieved in a way,' Gladys, maid at the big house, told us when she dropped in later. 'They were talking about it when I was handing the tureens round at luncheon.

'It was that mine disaster in Canada, see. They knew Miss Verity had gone to the West to join your Davey, and, not

260

knowing exactly where she was, they were afraid she might be dead. Knowing she was safe brought them to their senses.'

'There was a time when she'd have been better off dead, as far as they were concerned, than marrying a common miner,' I said.

'Don't be bitter, Gwen, *fach*.' Mam gave me a reproving look. 'Your father and I were against the marriage in the beginning, too. A gentile-reared girl, who had never done an honest day's work in her life. What sort of wife would she make for an ordinary working man?

'Still, I changed my mind, too, when I knew Davey was safe.' Mam smiled. 'So thankful I was, he could have married the Queen of Sheba for all I cared! We have only one life to live, and if Verity Morgan is Davey's choice, well, we must abide by it.'

'That is how the Morgans feel,' Gladys said softly. 'And now they are pleased because an old friend of Mr

Morgan gave the wedding reception for Verity. Now all is forgiven and they are talking about sending wedding presents.'

'Her poor mother,' Mam put in. 'Missing her only daughter's wedding like that.'

★ ★ ★

The following day, a cordial note came from Mrs Morgan, inviting Mam to call and take tea. So Mam duly put on her 'best bib and tucker', and went to Cwmbran House on the appointed day.

'We shall never be bosom pals,' she told me. 'But the woman is trying to make the best of a bad job, and I must play my part. There may come a day when Davey and his wife will return to Wales, and it will be important then for the two families to be on good terms.'

My mother was showing more courage than I would have done. They might be related through marriage, but Mrs Morgan was the lady of the manor.

My father and brothers had worked for her husband, and my sister had been a servant in their household! But still, when it came down to it, they had both suffered the same sort of shock when their children eloped.

When Mam came home, she was full of praise for Mrs Morgan, who had done her best to be cordial. A dainty tea had been served, and although Mam was not partial to China tea, she had managed to drink it.

'Although I almost choked, mind you, when Gladys came in, winking at me and grinning like a Cheshire cat.' Mam laughed at the memory. 'The poor wench — Madam saw her and chibbed her about it. 'Why are you making those dreadful faces, Roberts?' she said. 'Really, Mrs Rees, one simply cannot find decent servants nowadays!''

'What did you say to that, Mam?' I asked, aghast.

'Oh, I said I understood that it might be a problem, and then she seemed to remember who I was and got a bit embarrassed. She offered to show me the conservatory after our tea and I agreed, so out we went.

'Lovely, those flowers are, Gwen, all the colours of the rainbow. I was hoping she would offer me some to bring home, but she did not.'

★   ★   ★

As the time drew near for Gladys and Megan's double wedding, we were all drawn into the excitement. Gladys was thrilled because her mistress had given her a nice beige crêpe de chine dress, complete with a rather floppy rose made of the same material.

'Usually the lady's maid gets all the things Mrs Morgan does not want,' she enthused, 'but she thought I might like to have this for the wedding. The only thing is, I am not to wear it anywhere near Cwmbran Hall afterwards.'

'It is very kind of Mrs Morgan, I am sure,' Mam said diplomatically. 'Elegant it is, and the colour will suit you very well, Gladys, *fach*.'

'Perhaps you could dye it? Or trim it differently?' I suggested. 'After the wedding, I mean. It's such lovely material — too good to waste.'

'I must get a hat to go with this,' Gladys added. 'And you, too, Megan. You cannot wear your old navy blue felt with your new costume.'

So Megan, Gladys and I went to visit the milliner, with Mari skipping beside us. She had begged to come as she had often peered into the window of Miss Arbuthnot's tiny shop, and longed to see inside. She told me that she yearned to be old enough to be able to put her hair up and let her skirts down.

'Do not wish your life away, *cariad*,' I told her, quoting Mam. 'Having a long skirt is no joke. How often have you seen me having to sponge the hem of mine after I have walked home on a wet day?'

The room was filled with little stands on which ready-made hats waited for prospective customers.

Miss Arbuthnot also made hats on request, and when we entered she was busily blocking the crown of a pretty straw on what looked like a large wooden mushroom on a pedestal.

She came forward then, to ask how she could help us, and we faced the delectable task of choosing hats for the wedding.

Holding up a sample of the fabric from which her costume was made, Megan quickly selected a matching navy blue boater. Then she sat down happily to go through drawers full of trimmings, ribbons and artificial flowers.

'You must have something pretty for your wedding,' said the romantic Miss Arbuthnot. 'It's easy enough to remove the bits and pieces later, if it is too fancy for the chapel.'

Gladys was less easy to please. She tried on a number of hats, most of them wildly unsuitable.

'What do you think of this one?' she

asked, clamping on a wheat-coloured straw, trimmed with daisies.

Mari gave a small giggle from behind her hand.

'It makes you look . . . ' she began, but was silenced by a warning look from me.

I knew full well what my pony-mad little sister had been about to blurt out! Mr Patten at Penybont Farm was fond of his horse and in summer the mare always wore a straw hat with a few flowers drooping over her nose. Dear old Gladys did look rather like an amiable horse!

'I think that Mari was going to say that the colour makes you look a bit pale,' I amended hastily. 'And that colour will not match your dress.'

In the end, Megan settled on a white bird's wing to trim her navy straw, thinking that the resulting confection would look well with her navy blue costume and high-necked white blouse.

For herself Gladys chose a rakish

little hat with a bow of striped blue ribbon.

'And I have just the thing here to pin on your frock,' Miss Arbuthnot told her, bringing out an artificial flower which matched the ribbon.

It cost an extra twopence, but Gladys pounced on it at once. She would wear it instead of the beige one which had come with her dress, for it would serve as the traditional 'something blue'.

Next came the problem of gloves and shoes.

Megan was planning to wear her existing gloves, much darned at the fingertips, but I talked her out of that by promising to give each girl a new pair as a wedding gift from me.

Much cheered, Megan decided to wear her little black buttoned boots, and nothing any of us could say would talk her out of it.

Mrs Morgan had given Gladys the shoes to go with the frock. They were very smart, but unluckily they were a size too small.

'Hobble into the chapel, you will, if you try to wear those things,' Megan told her.

'I will not wear my old boots to get married in,' Gladys said. 'I will take them to Price the cobbler and ask him to stretch them.'

Because we were not invited to the wedding ceremony — the girls were sticking to their plan of having just the two couples at the chapel with the Reverend Mr Parry — I did not have to worry about new clothes for the day.

Mam and I had promised to go next door to serve the guests at the reception, and would be wearing aprons over our Sunday best in any case.

I was glad that I would be helping out on such a happy occasion, so when Llew came round to speak to Dada I gave him a friendly smile, which he may have taken the wrong way.

I told him that Dada had gone out but should be back at any moment and he smiled, neither put up nor down.

'I have been thinking,' he said, 'about

this double wedding — '

'Yes, I am glad that Megan has her chance at last. She looked after Mamgu for so long.'

'Indeed, Gwen,' he agreed. 'Two of the Roberts family getting married at the same time — so why not make it three?'

'You have someone in mind?' I laughed, to disguise my sinking heart.

'Perhaps we might make a go of it?' he wondered. 'We have known each other all our lives and . . . '

' . . . and I am still engaged to Bryn Edwards,' I finished, praying for Dada to come home and put a stop to this conversation. I liked Llew and did not want to hurt him, but I had no feelings for him.

'Oh, well . . . It was just a thought, Gwen.' He was flustered, his face reddening.

'You know, Llew,' I began, 'Dilys has always been soft on you.'

'Has she?' He brightened at that. 'I didn't know.'

He looked at me, amazed, before turning on his heel and leaving the house.

I watched him march briskly down the street with a new spring in his step — and wondered what I had let my friend in for!

★ ★ ★

On the big day, Olwen shut herself in the front room, muttering that she would not go next door to extend her good wishes to the two brides and their grooms, even though she had been invited.

'You might enjoy yourself,' Mam told her. 'Most of the staff from Cwmbran House are coming — girls you worked with when you were there. I am sure they would be glad to see you.'

'There will be questions if I go. Do I like my glamorous job? Do I have a young man?' Olwen pouted. 'I don't want anyone to know that I have given up my job, and the man I loved turned

271

out to be a rotter.'

'Na, na, perhaps not,' Mam admitted. 'You stay here, then, *cariad*, and we will bring you back a nice bit of cake.'

Megan and Gladys set off for the chapel, dressed in all their new finery. Gladys was hobbling along in her smart shoes and I was afraid that she would start married life with a fine crop of blisters!

I went next door to set out the food, leaving Mam behind to put the finishing touches to a trifle.

I was surprised when a knock came at the door, but supposed that one of the guests had mistaken the time and had come too early.

Rather annoyed, I flung it open, and nearly collapsed when I saw who was standing on the step. It was Bryn!

'Hello, Gwen!' he said, smiling.

Then I was in his arms, laughing and crying at the same time.

'How did you get here?' I managed to say. 'The last I heard, you had no money for your passage. Did the school trustees manage to pay you after all?'

'Not yet.' He shook his head. 'But I'm sure they will give me what they owe me in time. They are very honest people. It was Gareth and Davey,' he explained. 'I had a loan from them. They're making good money in the mine and have nowhere to spend it. They were glad to do something for their sister, they said.'

So this was the surprise packet that the boys were sending me! I thought that my heart would burst for joy.

'We will not let anything put off our wedding a second time,' Bryn told me. 'We cannot be married right away because I have no means of supporting a wife. But I will find a job somewhere, even if it is not in teaching. Then I will get a place to live and we can be married in the spring.'

'Why not right away? I know that Mam and Dada would let us have the front room, where the boys used to sleep.'

'We will start married life on the

273

right foot, *cariad*,' Bryn told me. 'I must first pay back the money I have borrowed. But never fear — it will all come right in the end, you will see.'

At that moment, I would have agreed to anything. Never could I feel happier than I did at that moment. The world seemed to stand still as we murmured all the little endearments that have been said by lovers down through the centuries . . .

But then there was no time to say more. The newly-married couples arrived, with the wedding guests close on their heels, and the house was filled with chatter and happy laughter.

★ ★ ★

They say that every bride is beautiful on her wedding day and it was true. Megan's face was alight with happiness, and even dear homely Gladys was pink and smiling under her pretty hat.

I seemed to feel Mamgu's presence in the room which had been hers for so long. Was it fanciful to imagine that she was smiling down benevolently on her two granddaughters on their day of days?

Dilys was beaming from the corner where she was waiting for Llew to bring her a glass of Mam's homemade metheglin with which to toast the bridal couples. He was being very attentive, and I could see that she was delighted. Her patience had paid off.

Bryn lifted his glass to me and I touched it lightly with mine. Until an hour ago, I had expected that this day would stir up painful memories for me but now everything was right with my world.

In just a few months, I would be marrying my own true love, and starting a new life with him, when the daffodils bloomed again in Cwmbran.

The End.

CHRISTMAS CHARADE

Kay Gregory

When Nina Petrov meets charismatic businessman Fenton Hardwick on a transcontinental train to Chicago, she sees him as the solution to her recurring Christmas problem. Every year her matchmaking father produces a different hopelessly unsuitable man for her to marry. Nina decides she needs a temporary fiancé to get him off her case, and Fen seems the perfect candidate for the job — until she makes the mistake of trying to pay him for his help . . .

A LETTER TO MY LOVE

Toni Anders

Devastated when Marcus married someone else, Sorrel resolved to devote her life to her toyshop and her invalid cousin, Alyse. However, when she meets Carl, the Bavarian woodcarver, it provides a romantic distraction — but Marcus's growing friendship with Alyse unsettles Sorrel. She is torn between her still-present love for Marcus, and her cousin's happiness. When Marcus's spiteful sister, Pamela, decides to repossess the toyshop for a wine bar, Sorrel decides to fight them both.

DOCTOR, DOCTOR

Chrissie Loveday

The arrival of a new doctor in a small Cornish hospital causes a stir, especially among the female members of staff. Lauren has worked hard to build her career, along with a protective shell to keep her emotions intact. She won't risk being hurt again, but Tom has other ideas . . . As they share the highs and lows of hospital life, they develop a mutual respect for each other's professional skills — but can there ever be more to their relationship?

YOURS FOR ETERNITY

Janet Whitehead

Danielle McMasters was haunted by the memory of the man she had loved and lost in a fatal car crash six years before. Ben was dead. So who, then, was the man watching her from across the room? His likeness was uncanny — it had to be Ben . . . hadn't it? But how could he have returned from the grave — and why was someone following her every move? The past was haunting her present, but how would it affect her future?

THE RETURN OF LORD RIVENHALL

Fenella Miller

Amelia Rivenhall is delighted when Richard arrives to claim the title left vacant by the sudden death of her father eighteen months previously. But when William also turns up, claiming that Richard is an impostor and that he is the real Lord Rivenhall, her troubles are just beginning. She discovers that when a huge inheritance is at stake, impostors and rogues will try anything to claim their money . . .